Praise for the

'This was a great find.
1960s England. Janie Ju
is a very likeable protagonist. A real page turner. I've already bought the next book in the series... hoping there will be many more to come.'

'I got straight into the story ... I really like the way the author depicted the 60s ...I felt as if I was there!'

'Intriguing detective story with lovely period setting and interesting characters. I'm looking forward to seeing what Janie Juke solves next.'

'Loved every page and didn't want to put it down. Can't wait until the next one in the series.'

'Thoroughly enjoyable book. Kept me interested till the end. Looking forward to the next one.'

'The glimpses into WW2 are particularly good. Solid writing, great story, and Janie as a character is growing on me. I hope there are more in the series.'

About the author

Isabella rediscovered her love of writing fiction during two happy years working on and completing her MA in Professional Writing.

The setting for the *Janie Juke* mystery series is based on the area where Isabella was born and lived most of her life. When she thinks of Tamarisk Bay she pictures her birthplace in St Leonards-on-Sea, East Sussex and its surroundings.

Aside from her love of words, Isabella has a love of all things caravan-like. She has enjoyed several years travelling in the UK and abroad. Now, Isabella and her husband run a small campsite in West Sussex.

Her faithful companion, Scottish terrier Hamish, is never far from her side.

Find out more about Isabella, her published books, as well as her forthcoming titles at: **www.isabellamuir.com** and follow Isabella on Twitter: **@SussexMysteries**

By the same author

THE TAPESTRY BAG
THE INVISIBLE CASE
THE FORGOTTEN CHILDREN
IVORY VELLUM: A COLLECTION OF SHORT STORIES

LOST PROPERTY

A JANIE JUKE MYSTERY

By Isabella Muir

Published in Great Britain
By Outset Publishing Ltd

Second edition published June 2018
First edition published December 2017

ISBN:1-872889-13-1

ISBN-13:978-1-872889-13-9

www.isabellamuir.com

Cover photo: by Wheres Lugo on Unsplash
Cover design: by Christoffer Petersen
Map of Tamarisk Bay: by Richard Whincop

It's autumn 1969, in a quiet seaside town in Sussex. Janie Juke has unravelled the mystery of *The Tapestry Bag* and now she has secrets on her mind...

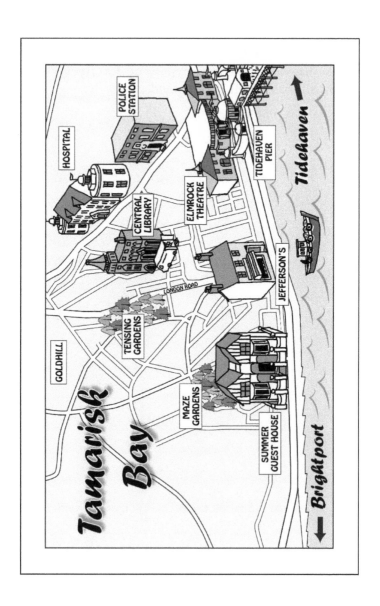

Chapter 1

'What's your definition of a secret?' I am sitting in dad's kitchen, at the Formica-covered table that has been the site of many of our important chats over the years.

'Let's have a think,' he says. 'Well, I suppose it's information that is not to be shared?'

'And a lie?'

'In essence, it's the same thing. A lie might be the words that are spoken in place of the secret, or the words that are not spoken. A lie can be the silence.'

A month ago I ended a search for a friend. A week ago I was asked to begin another search. But this time for a stranger.

'What's this talk about secrets and lies? Is there something you don't want to tell Greg?' My dad can't see my face, but he has always been able to read my mind.

'Yes, I made a sort of promise.'

'When you married him?' dad smiles.

My hesitation in replying doesn't go unnoticed.

'Sorry, I shouldn't tease you,' he continues. 'You mean a few weeks ago, when you agreed to settle down and plan for the arrival of your baby. Has something happened to make you change your mind?'

'I've been approached by someone to track down a woman.'

'And you're wondering whether to tell Greg?'

'Yes, he worries so much. I know it's only because he cares, but even so...'

'Ah,' dad says and smiles, small creases appearing around the edges of his eyes that I haven't noticed before. 'Is that husband of yours still enjoying his new job?'

'He loves it. He's learning the building trade and I'm learning the vocabulary. I can now give you the low-down on the importance of unbridged cavities, while being able to spot efflorescence at a glance. It's fascinating. Mr Mowbray says Greg will be building a wall before Christmas. Fastest apprenticeship known to man.'

'And your apprenticeship?'

'Exactly. I have a sneaky feeling I could be good at this investigating business.'

Some may say investigating is an odd pastime for a librarian and perhaps pastime is the wrong word. The truth is, I appear to excel at sticking my nose into other people's business. Much of the blame can be laid at the door of Agatha Christie. From an early age her books filled my shelves at home and now I have even greater access to them, via the library. I've learned a lot from Poirot.

'It doesn't have to be a competition, princess. You both have a chance to learn a new trade. Although being a competent librarian is important in itself.'

'I know, you're right.'

'Maybe Greg needs more time, to get used to the idea?'

'I don't have more time. Bean will be here in a few months. This case needs to be well and truly solved long before then. If it's to be solved at all.'

In the first couple of months of my pregnancy I discovered my little embryo resembled a kidney bean. I told Greg and the name stuck. Heaven help the poor child when it's born if we forget the name is temporary, or if we haven't settled on a new one.

'Can you tell me anything about this new case?' dad asks.

'One of my library customers has asked for my help.'

On the days when I don't help dad, I run the local mobile library. I have a regular route and plenty of regular customers. Mr Furness was a newcomer to the library and it was on his third visit to investigate the non-fiction shelves when he approached me to do some investigating of a different kind.

'He wants your help to find a woman? Is that all you know? What else has he told you about her?'

'Very little. There appears to be a mystery regarding a left luggage ticket.'

'Intriguing.'

'Mm, maybe.'

'What's the ticket got to do with the missing woman? Has this man given you the ticket? Has he asked you to do something with it?'

'In a way, yes. You know the lost property box I keep in the van?'

Since I've been in charge of the library van, I've gathered some fascinating items of lost property. Customers arriving on wet days frequently become so immersed in their browsing that they leave with their minds full of new stories and their hands empty of their umbrella - or walking stick. You would think that, once outside, with the rain pelting down, they would hastily return to salvage their winter protection. But my collection of six umbrellas and three walking sticks appears to prove otherwise. I keep the smaller items of lost treasure in a cardboard box under the counter in the van. The box contains an assortment of spectacles, gloves and mittens, a silk scarf, a snuff box and my favourite item, a single pink ankle sock - an adult's one at that. Now and again I wonder whether its owner will be hanging their washing on the line one day and have a sudden recollection of the day when they called into the mobile library and left a sock behind. It's a fanciful thought though, as it has remained in my box for almost a year now.

Dad waits calmly for me to continue. 'Talk me through it, if you like. It might help to clarify your thoughts,' he says.

'Okay, I'll refresh our drinks first though, shall I?'

With drinks made and the plate of digestives topped up, I recount to dad as much as I know about Hugh Furness.

On his first visit to the library I guessed that Mr Furness was a stranger to Tamarisk Bay, or at least I hadn't seen him before. As he walked through the van doorway he dipped down slightly, the smart Trilby that was perched on his head just missing the frame. Once inside, he held himself upright, all six feet something and removed his hat. He reminded me of an actor. He kept his dark grey gaberdine mac fastened firmly around his muscular frame, the belt pulled in around his middle, like a neatly wrapped parcel. The deep red silk cravat around his neck reflected its colour on his chin, giving him a ruddy glow. Perhaps in his younger days he could have been a Robert Mitchum, or Gregory Peck.

He had only been in the van a short while, when the comfortable silence was disturbed by the raucous sound of a coughing fit. Once Mr Furness started coughing it seemed he could not stop. He was distressed, I was distressed and the result was that, as soon as he could catch his breath, he put his Trilby back on his head and left, embarrassed perhaps at the scene he had caused. A few minutes later I noticed he had dropped a left luggage ticket.

Reuniting the left luggage ticket with its rightful owner would appear to be the easiest thing in the world. However, when Mr Furness returned a few days later, I explained about the ticket and offered it to him, but he denied all knowledge of the little slip of paper.

We all know about the concept of 'third time lucky', although its origin is yet to be proved. Nevertheless, superstition, or folklore, notwithstanding, it was on the gentleman's third visit when I was able to establish the connection between the left luggage ticket and my enigmatic customer.

Dad has been listening intently. 'What did he say to you? Did he explain why he'd told you the ticket wasn't his?'

'Not really. He just said, *I lied*.'

'That brings us back to our conversation earlier, about secrets and lies.'

'Exactly.'

'I don't like the idea that this Mr Furness has started off his dealings with you by lying. It doesn't bode well.'

'Mm, good point. Well, I've asked him to call back next Monday. Hopefully I'll be able to pin him down and find out more.'

'Remember to read between the lines - that's where you'll find the clues.'

'Now you sound like Poirot,' I say, giving dad a hug.

On Monday morning, as I park the van in my usual place on Milburn Avenue, there is Hugh Furness, waiting.

'Good morning, Mrs Juke,' he says, stepping into the van and removing his hat. His hair is pure white. I've noticed it before, but now everything about him has added significance. He may be my first official client. He is old enough to be going grey, perhaps, but white? I make a mental note to write my observation in my notebook.

'Hello there, you're nice and prompt,' I say.

He smiles. It's the first time I've seen him smile and it surprises me how much it changes his demeanour.

'Thank you for agreeing to help me. Where shall we start?' he says. There's a briskness in his voice, an urgency; this is not a man to be messed with.

'One step at a time, Mr Furness. I haven't agreed to anything yet.'

The smile fades away, leaving an expression that could be irritation. Equally, I know so little about this man, my attempts at reading his body language are as tricky as an Eskimo trying to understand smoke signals.

'There's a lot I need to ask you and plenty you'll want to share with me, I'm sure?' I say.

I can't tell whether he agrees, or if he thinks I have already overstepped some imaginary line. 'Let's arrange a meeting, shall we? Somewhere quiet.'

He raises an eyebrow.

'I know, libraries are quiet, but this is my place of work. We would have to stop speaking every time someone walks in.'

As if on cue, the door opens. Mrs Latimer, one of my regulars, is returning a couple of books. She approaches the counter, seemingly unaware she is interrupting. She wants to chat about her son, who is recovering from a nasty cold.

'Of course, Bobby's asthma is worse than ever,' she says. 'I'll have to keep him off school again, but I'm worried he'll never catch up. That's why I thought I would borrow a couple more books. We do a few lessons at home, but he's not keen. Says he'd rather be watching television. I ask you. When I was a youngster there was just the wireless and that would only go on for the news.'

I smile and nod, trying not to encourage her too much. While I'm listening to her chatting, Mr Furness moves away to browse the bookshelves. Moments later, as Mrs Latimer transfers her attention to the children's book section, he returns to the counter.

'Case in point,' he says.

'Yes. Let's choose a meeting place. Do you know the town well?'

'Not very.'

'There are some gardens, in the Maze Road area of town. I can show you on a street map, if you like?'

I take out a map of Tamarisk Bay and spread it over the counter.

'Just here,' I point. 'There's a little café, well in truth it's more of a shack. But if the weather is bad we can sit inside, if not we can wander around the gardens and chat. Does that sound okay?'

An imaginary conversation is playing in my mind. Greg is glaring at me in horror as I tell him I'm going to be wandering around Tensing Gardens with a man I barely know. Fortunately, Greg won't have to worry because I won't be telling him, at least not yet.

'Tensing Gardens is fine,' Mr Furness says, bringing my attention back to the here and now.

'Tomorrow afternoon? 4pm?'

'Certainly. Thank you, my dear,' he holds his hand out to shake mine. It feels as though I am agreeing a formal contract with a man I know nothing about, to undertake a job I have little experience of. Greg would call me impetuous, dad might use the word impulsive. My reckoning is that I'm just a little crazy.

'This is just a preliminary chat, you do understand? I don't know if I'll be able to help you.'

'I have nothing to lose,' he says, looking directly at me. His voice is firm and yet there is a hesitancy about him.

'Tomorrow then,' I say.

He nods, takes his hat from the counter and leaves.

My only other customer returns to the counter with her books.

'Didn't the gentleman find what he was looking for?' she asks.

'I'm not sure,' I reply.

Chapter 2

On the two days of each working week when I'm not running the mobile library I help my dad out. My dad is a gifted physiotherapist. He is also blind. He tells me that losing one sense has helped to accentuate those remaining. After his accident, the physiotherapists helped him so much with his struggles to regain independence that once he was ready to seek a new career, physiotherapy was the obvious one. There's no doubt that his patients would confirm he made the right choice. He has a waiting list of customers, all of them keen for his expertise, which doesn't only deal with their physical ailments. He is a careful listener, never judging and often offering wise words. He sends patients on their way, not just with an easier shoulder or back, but with a happier heart as well.

On Tuesdays and Thursdays there is paperwork to complete, housework to keep on top of and the fridge and cupboards to check. If I didn't remind him, then healthy eating would not be high on dad's list of priorities. Charlie also benefits from all the fuss. Charlie is dad's German Shepherd dog. Wherever dad is, there is Charlie, who is loyal, hardworking and intelligent. Well, I suppose that goes for both of them.

'Okay if I leave a bit early today?' I say. 'There are plenty of clean towels ready for your appointments tomorrow and I've made a stew and left it in the fridge. You can't live on salad and sandwiches now we've seen the last of summer.'

We haven't spoken any more about my possible new case and I haven't mentioned my planned meeting with Mr Furness, but that doesn't mean dad won't have his suspicions.

'Beef stew? Sounds good. You will be careful, princess,' he says, as I grab my coat from the back of the kitchen chair.

'I'm always careful.'

'You know what I'm saying.'

'I will, I promise. See you Thursday,' I say, kissing him on his cheek. 'Bye Charlie, look after my old man, for me.'

'Not so much of the old.'

'You'll be Grandpa before long, so you'd better get used to it.'

Before his accident dad was a detective and, by all accounts, a pretty good one. So, what with Poirot's help and dad's advice, I have more than a head start.

Autumn has arrived in Tensing Gardens. The muted shades of amber, red and gold are brightened by the afternoon sunshine. The paths are covered with acorns and conkers. A grey squirrel is up ahead of me, its bushy tail reminding me of the fur collar of one of mum's coats. I shake the thought away, as I watch the squirrel sprint up one of the trees, its mouth bulging with an acorn treasure.

As I approach the rickety shack I spot Mr Furness. He is pacing up and down. Once again a prompt arrival. I slow my pace so that I can study him for a few moments. His strides are even, almost a march and as he reaches the end of the little path in front of the café, he turns on his heel. There is nothing casual about his movement. I'm close enough to see his forehead is creased with a frown, which immediately dissipates when he sees me approach.

'Good afternoon, Mrs Juke,' he says.

'Janie.'

'Ah, yes, I'm Hugh. You're right, if we're to be working together there's no need for formalities.'

'One step at a time, Hugh.'

'Of course, of course.'

'Let's take a seat inside, shall we? At least while there are no other customers.'

'Can I get you a cup of tea?'

'Er, no, coffee please.'

I can no longer stomach tea. Even the smell of it makes me queasy. In recent weeks I am also off spicy foods and cucumber. I'd always assumed the arrival of a new baby would require a change of routine, but I hadn't anticipated a change of diet. All this and Bean hasn't even been born yet.

We step inside the shack and I'm reminded of the woodcutter's cottage in one of my favourite fairy tales. Hugh walks over to the long wooden table that serves as a counter and orders our drinks. Everything about the woman behind the counter is round. She has a moon-shaped face and a comfortably large middle. Even her hair is wound tightly around and pinned into a little bun at the back of her head that reminds me of a doughnut. She is resting one arm on a walking stick, which appears to be there more from habit than necessity, because when she brings our drinks over to us she walks with certainty. A reminder that all is not what it appears at first.

'What would you like to know?' Hugh removes our drinks from the tray and carefully measures two teaspoons of sugar into his cup. As he stirs the sugar the table wobbles, spilling some of our drinks into the saucers. Either the table legs are uneven, or the floor below us is as rickety as the shack itself.

'I'm sorry, I didn't mean to ...I'll get a paper serviette,' he says.

'It wasn't your fault, it was the table.'

Perhaps he is not used to clandestine assignations with young women, or perhaps there is another reason for his nervousness. He places the serviette inside the saucer to mop up the spilt liquid and then he begins to cough. I've heard him cough this way before. The first time he came into the library van he had a coughing fit, which ended with rasping and wheezing. Now it appears he is suffering again. He struggles to catch his breath and the elderly woman who served us brings over a glass of water.

'You alright there, ducky?' she asks him.

He doesn't respond as he tries to calm his breathing, but after a few minutes the episode passes and he is settled again.

'That sounds nasty,' I say, 'is the doctor helping with medicine?'

He shakes his head. 'I'm sorry, let's start again. I'm grateful you've agreed to meet me.'

'You said I could help you, but I need some background. So, if you don't mind, I've prepared some questions.' I take my notebook and pencil out of my duffel bag.

If I had been a Brownie or a Girl Guide, perhaps I would have learned the motto, *Be prepared.* Instead Poirot taught me. His methodical approach to detecting has become mine. I've added to my toolkit since my search for Zara. My notebook forms the basis of it, but now I am the proud owner of an Instamatic camera. There were several occasions over the last few months when a snapshot would have proved useful, a visual record to support my note-taking.

With my detective's toolkit at the ready, I am prepared to take on a new challenge. New assignment, new notebook, new focus.

My questions are listed under five separate headings - *Who?, What?, Why?, Where?, When?* - a page for each. Every possible detail about the person I'm seeking is critical, but

I also need to know more about Mr Furness and the *'What?'* of my investigations. What is the purpose of the search? What is Mr Furness doing in Tamarisk Bay?

Too many questions to tackle in one sitting, but at least today I can make a start. I open my notebook and flick through the various sections. I decide to start with the *Who?*

'You'd like some help tracking down a friend?' My pencil is poised.

'Yes.'

'What is your friend's name?'

'Dorothy Elm. At least that was her name when I knew her, she may have married since.'

'And what is your relationship to Dorothy?'

'I don't have one. Not now at least.'

'She was your friend?'

'Yes.'

I make a few notes on the *Who?* page and he watches me.

'How long is it since you've seen her? When were you friends?'

'During the war.'

'And you haven't seen her since?'

'No.'

'We're talking twenty years ago?'

'Twenty-five actually. I last saw her in 1944.'

'Forgive me, Mr Furness. Hugh. But why now?'

He glances down at his cup and saucer, at the tea that is cooling and remains undrunk.

'My wife died. Last year.'

'I'm so sorry. That's very sad. You must miss her.'

A bubble of indignation begins to surface. I am ready to confront Greg with an unfair question. *'So, if I died, how long would you wait before tracking down an old sweetheart?'* I am so focused on imagining Greg's response that I miss the next thing Hugh says.

'Pardon?' I ask him.

'She had been ill for a long time.'

'It must have been a difficult time for you both.'

I'm not sure I want to continue with the conversation. I'm already annoyed with Hugh Furness and I haven't even reached the *When?, Where?,* or significantly, the *What? s*ections of my notebook. What does he think I can do that he can't? If you want to track down an old friend, why on earth would you enlist the help of a twenty-four-year-old librarian? A pregnant one as well, come to that.

'Shall we call a halt for now, Hugh? I need to get back to fix my husband's supper.'

He remains motionless, his face blank. I wonder if he has heard me. I stand, so that he gets the message that our conversation is over, at least for now.

'I loved my wife very much,' he says.

'I'm pleased to hear that.'

I sit again, prepared to give him the benefit of the doubt.

'And you have already checked the obvious places?'

He gives me a quizzical look, but says nothing.

'The telephone directory?'

'Yes, of course. There are three Elms listed in the local directory, but none with the initial D. Besides, I doubt Dorothy would have a telephone and, as I explained, she may have married. You must understand that I wouldn't be asking you if it was as simple as looking in a book.' His jaw tenses and there is frustration in his voice. 'I really need to find her.'

'Why is that Hugh?'

'I think she may be in danger. That's the point, you see. I'm scared that if I don't find her and warn her, then something very bad may happen to her.'

'Shouldn't you involve the police?'

'They are not always helpful, are they? I think you know what I mean.'

He's referring to my search for Zara.

'Okay,' I say, 'so take me back to 1944.'

He closes his eyes and I wait. A few moments pass and then he speaks.

Chapter 3

1944

She saw the dog first. It was matching his master's pace, stride for stride. At least, it was trying to, but not entirely succeeding, as its legs were so short. Short, but willing. Every few minutes the man turned, perhaps to check the dog was still there, perhaps to persuade it that it wasn't a hopeless cause.

The man slowed his pace, the dog caught up. She could have watched them for hours, but she needed to scrub up and get back to the farmhouse for tea.

At the thought of tea she was reminded how hungry she was. She was used to the physical labour now, but still surprised by the appetite that came along with it. They were luckier than most. There was always plenty to eat, vegetables picked that day and made into warming hotpots. Bread was baked daily and she loved the saltiness of the home-churned butter from the dairy herd. She remembers too readily the restrictions of rationing. Before coming to work as a land girl she often spent her mornings queuing for the basics, returning home with barely enough to make a meal. But here on the farm there was no need for powdered egg, the chickens roamed freely, providing more than enough for all the workers.

Next day, at around the same time, she saw him again. There was such a sense of abandon in the way he strolled, with the little dog trotting beside him. Any pretence at freedom these days had to be grabbed, if only for a moment or two.

Then for several days there was no sign of him. There had been talk of successful missions over Germany. Key sites had been flattened, but there had been casualties too, on both sides. She prayed he wasn't one of the pilots who had lost his life.

She didn't even know his name.

Then the day came when he was there again, with his Scottish Terrier trotting beside him. She could have literally jumped with the joy of seeing them both.

During the days when he hadn't appeared, when she'd waited as long as possible before going back to the farmhouse for her tea, she made a pledge to herself. The next time she saw him she would speak to him. Now the moment was here.

'May I pat your dog?' she said. Her voice startled him, he hadn't noticed her approach. He stopped walking and his dog continued for a few paces, sniffing among the leaves.

'What's his name?'

'Scottie,' he said. 'Original, eh?' When he smiled, his face took on a glow. His eyes were dark, the colour of blueberries, his hair light brown and wavy. She imagined his mother teasing the knots from his babyhood curls.

'Will you walk with us a while?' he said. He noticed her hesitation, even though it was momentary. 'We're not going far.'

She didn't want to admit that she knew his route all too well. She'd watched them skirt around the edge of the field, into the first part of the wood and emerge again on the other side, maybe ten minutes later.

She was conscious of her untidy hair, wisps of it escaping from the plait that wound around her head. Her hands were muddy from the planting and she was certain she smelled of sweat. She put all her energy into the farm work, taking a pride in it, knowing she was helping to feed a nation. A nation at war.

Every week since her arrival she had written to her brother, reassuring him that she was justified in making the move. Her home was a little over fifty miles away, too far for him to visit and she missed him.

'Will Scottie chase a ball?' she asked.

'He doesn't really run, he's more of a plodder.'

'I'd like to join you on your walk, but I have to be back at 5pm sharp, for tea. Terrible trouble, if not.'

'That's a shame,' he said, any hope in his expression fading.

'Perhaps tomorrow? If you're here again? A little earlier maybe, so there's time for a stroll?'

'If I can, it's difficult to plan from one day to the next. I'm sure you understand?'

She glanced sideways at him. Now that she was closer to him she could absorb all the detail of his uniform, without appearing to stare. The light caught the polish on the buttons, on his boots.

'You're working here on the farm?' he asked.

She nodded. 'Yes, I've joined the Women's Land Army, I'm a land girl.'

'Good for you, I mean it's vital work you're doing and hard too. Have you farmed before?'

'No, I love it though. I didn't realise how satisfying it would be. Planting tiny seeds and watching them grow. Harvesting crops that appear from nothing. Just the sun, the rain and the goodness from the soil. It's all in the preparation, you know.'

'Isn't everything?' he said, laugh lines appearing at the edges of his eyes.

The next day he kept his word and arrived a little earlier, with Scottie bouncing along beside him.

'He's taken a shine to you,' he said, as she bent down to greet the terrier. 'As soon as I told him where we were going, there was an added spring in his step.'

They walked and chatted about the farm and about dogs, carefully avoiding any mention of the recent spate of bombings that had been terrifying everyone on the peninsula.

'Who watches out for Scottie when you're on a mission?' she asked.

'We help each other out. Plenty of chaps have dogs, a brisk walk helps to while away the time between shouts. Although I'll admit that Scottie and brisk are not words I would often use together.'

The conversation was easy and light. She told him what she had learned about the seasons and the weather, how much she enjoyed being part of a team. 'The timing is critical, whether you are planting or harvesting, a heavy downpour at the wrong time can destroy months of work. Look at these hands,' she said, holding them out in front of her, 'not likely to pass for a lady with these, eh?' They laughed together. When they reached the end of the farm track she wished they could do it all again.

'There's a dance tomorrow night. In the village hall. Are you going?' he asked.

She could feel the heat in her face, she hoped he wouldn't notice.

'Yes, a bunch of us land girls are going.'

'We're going too, I mean some of the squadron. So, perhaps I'll see you there?'

She smiled as he held out his hand.

She chose the same dress she had worn the last time she went to the village hall dance, but it didn't matter because he wasn't there last time. She would have noticed if he had been.

The red and white striped material was smart, not showy. It was nipped in around the middle, accentuating her trim waist. She wore a navy cardigan around her shoulders and was relieved her only pair of elegant shoes were navy too.

He had only ever seen her hair up, braided and wound around her head. It was easier to have it out of the way when she was working in the fields. But for the dance she would wear it long and loose, kept in place with a white scarf tied like a band, keeping her fringe from falling into her eyes. One of the girls had shown the rest of them how to use beetroot to redden their lips. There was little or no chance of laying your hands on lipstick, or mascara come to that. No hope for stockings either. Some of the girls coloured their legs with cold tea, or gravy browning, but all she ever bothered with was a line drawn up the back to look like a stocking seam.

The night of the dance there was a chill in the air, so there was no need to pinch her cheeks to bring the colour to them. As she walked into the village hall she felt flushed, perhaps with the warmth generated by the crowd of chaps and girls who were already taking a turn on the dance floor, or perhaps by the anticipation of taking a turn herself, with him.

He strode over to her as soon as he spotted her arrive. Taking her hand he led her into the centre of the dancing crowd, nudging past other couples, creating space for the two of them. He had great rhythm and was light on his feet. All around the walls of the hall someone had hung brightly coloured bunting, which flapped around as the dancers moved, churning up the air with their lively steps.

They tried the Jitterbug and the Lindy Hop.

The chairs and tables were pushed against the walls, leaving the floor area free. A raised platform created a stage for the band. Two men in air force uniform provided the music, one on the piano, the other with a trombone. Beside them stood a young girl with a confident voice, lilting and clear.

They both hummed along to the tunes. 'Do you know the words?' she asked him. He shook his head and laughed. At the end of the evening she was ready to collapse.

'Not harder than ploughing, surely?' he said, pouring them both a glass of lemonade.

'Faster though, definitely,' she said.

During the evening neither of them had spoken much to the other chaps and girls in their group. It was only when Maud came over to remind her it was time to leave that she even remembered they were there.

'I have to go now,' she said, 'we get into trouble if we're in later than 10pm.'

'Curfew?' he said. 'I hope you don't think I'm being forward, but my friend has a boat. It's a small fishing boat, moored in the harbour. We could meet on it, tomorrow if you like. Are you free tomorrow?'

'We have every Sunday free, there's church first, but afterwards...'

He put a hand up to her face and brushed a loose hair away from her cheek.

'After church then,' he said.

She cycled to the harbour and wondered how she would recognise the boat. There were several tied up along the quay. But he was there before her, waiting on the beach, with Scottie sitting beside him. They were both gazing out to sea. Seagulls were circling overhead, cawing loudly.

'Are they waiting for you to catch them a fish?' she said. Scottie gave a little bark and ran to her. She picked him up and hugged him close to her. As soon as she set him down again he started running in circles, with his tail wagging vigorously.

'You see, he loves you,' he said.

She couldn't stop herself blushing and hoped he hadn't noticed, or that he would put it down to the brisk onshore wind, bringing the blood to her cheeks.

'What will you catch?' she asked him.

'We'll be lucky to catch anything, I'm not much good. What about you?'

'Never fished before in my life.'

'Poor seagulls.'

He helped her to step into the boat, then lifted Scottie in. Using the wooden oars, he pushed the boat away from the quay, having untied the rope that was holding it in place. The tide was high and the wind churned up the water. They bobbed along and she laughed each time a wave crashed against the side of the boat, splashing them both. When they were far enough out, he prepared the rod and line, added bait to the hook, then cast it out into the water.

'Now what?' she said.

'We wait.'

'How long?'

'Until we get a bite, or until we get bored.'

'Or until curfew,' she said and laughed.

'My friend tells me there's bass to be had, if we're lucky.'

He cast the line out again and again, but they weren't to be lucky with fish that day.

'Next Sunday?' he asked, as she stepped out of the boat on their return to the harbour. 'If I'm not on a mission, of course.'

This time when they parted he kissed her on the cheek. His lips were warm against her chilled face.

'I'd like that,' she said.

Throughout that spring they met several times on the little fishing boat. To pass the time, while they waited for the fish to bite, she read poetry to him. Some days, when the wind was brisk, she had to raise her voice to be heard above the crash and splash of the water. At first she selected snippets from Emily Dickinson and Keats. Then, as she grew in confidence, she shared some of her own. She had played around with words since she was a child. By putting a pencil to a sheet of paper she could create an imaginary world, several in fact. Her poems chimed with the swell of the sea.

He struggled to reconcile the different sides of this woman, who on their walks breathed fun and frivolity. Then, when they were in the little boat, he would listen to her soft voice reciting lyrical rhythms and rhymes, close his eyes, and sense another person entirely.

They had spoken briefly about their past, the lives they had left behind to join in the fight for freedom. Both of them had lost close friends in the bombings. She lived in fear that one day she would receive news that the house she was born in had been crushed, and her brother along with it. But thankfully, so far the news had not arrived.

Most of the time he was overly cheerful, making jokes, as if to chase away the blackness. She could tell the days when he had flown a tough mission. All the sorties were difficult, but when he returned and others didn't, those were the worst.

The poetry calmed them, giving them time to think about love. A small word that neither of them would use, not yet. They both understood that the war may not allow

the roots to spread and grow. Each day had to be lived as
though it was their last.

Chapter 4

Hugh stops speaking and draws a long breath. The tea shack feels colder than before. Hugh has spoken of romance, but there is something about his story that chills me. I have remained silent throughout his story, focusing on the detail, ensuring I absorb every nuance. I wait, uncertain as to whether he intends to continue. He is gazing down at his unfinished drink. Then he shakes his head, as though he is responding to some internal argument. Finally, he looks across at me.

'It must be difficult for you, reliving those times?' I say. 'It sounds as though your relationship with Dorothy was very special.'

He nods.

'And your RAF base was...?'

'Longmere, fifty miles due west from here, along the coast.'

He hesitates. Earlier he was in full flow, describing his meeting with Dorothy, their time at the dance and their fishing escapades, but now it's as if he has exhausted all the happy memories and what remains is a dark pit that he wants to avoid climbing into. Then, suddenly, he stands up. 'Can we call a halt for now? You must be needing to get home. I've taken up enough of your time,' he says.

'I can see you're tired, but there's a lot more I need to know before I can pursue your case. Shall we fix another meeting?'

'I'll call into the library,' he says.

Before I can respond, he dons his Trilby and holds his hand out to shake mine. I've barely had time to put my notebook and pencil back in my duffel bag, when I hear the door to the shack bang closed. Hugh has departed.

Overnight I park the library van in the Central Library car park. On my library mornings I walk the fifteen minutes or so from home and call into the staff office to pick up the van keys. Occasionally, when the warmth of my bed beckons, I leave home later and catch the bus. It saves me five minutes or so, if it's on time. I guess as Bean starts to hamper my progress over the coming winter months, the bus option will win on a few more occasions.

When I arrive to pick up the library van on Friday morning, Hugh is standing there in the car park. This time he is wearing a navy blazer and dark grey trousers and as he turns to greet me I notice the same red cravat tucked inside his open-necked shirt.

'Can we meet again? In Tensing Gardens?' he says. 'Today would suit me, do you have a lunch break?' His tone is polite, but official.

'I tend to snack at my desk, well, at the counter. The next time I'm free is Tuesday.'

'Time is of the essence. Each day that passes, the situation becomes more critical. You do understand the need for urgency?'

He stands in front of me, ram-rod straight, not leaning more on one foot than another, as so many people do. I wonder if it's down to his military training.

I remember Greg mentioning a darts match. He never wants me there, although I tag along now and then. 'I could make it this evening, if you're free?' I pause, trying to select a meeting place that is less lonely than the gardens on an autumn evening, but somewhere we can talk undisturbed. 'How about the café on the Pier? It closes at 8pm, but before that it should be quiet enough, most people will be home having supper.'

He nods and takes out a notepad from his top jacket pocket, together with a fountain pen. 'Café on the Pier, 7pm,' he repeats, as he writes.

Fridays are always busy, with people wanting to choose their reading material for the weekend. Given the weather forecast for this particular October weekend, the stream of borrowers leads me to believe they are all planning a quiet couple of days snuggled up in front of a fire.

Having dropped the van back to the Central Library car park, I make my way home and change. There's just enough time for toast and Marmite, before I leave to walk down towards the seafront. With the wind blasting, even along the back streets, I wrap myself up in so many layers that Bean's growing bump is barely visible.

The seafront runs from west to east, starting in Tamarisk Bay and ending at Tidehaven Old Town, with the Pier situated about half-way along the promenade. Sadly, there's no evidence remaining of the second pier, that dad and Aunt Jessica often talked about. They both spent happy summers in the penny arcades of the Victorian structure, which was apparently hailed as a masterpiece of design and construction, before it was badly damaged by severe gales during the Second World War. Then, just a few months later, it was totally destroyed by a major fire. But at least we still have Tidehaven Pier, with its dance hall and the Pier Café.

The café is circular in its design, with large windows all around that make the most of the sea views. Its position means it has taken the brunt of the weather over decades, resulting in gales blasting through the metal-framed windows. There are no cosy corners to retreat to, so when I arrive I'm concerned to see Hugh seated at a table close to a window, on the east side of the café. This evening a strong north-easterly is blowing and, for a girl who is even cold in August, I can see his seat selection is going to cause a problem.

'Hello there,' I say, as I glance around for a preferable position. 'Do you mind if we move? It's draughty everywhere, but maybe over this side?' I point to a table next to a window that appears to be well taped up with draughtproof tape. I make a mental note to remind Greg not to buy the cheapest strip when he gets around to doing our windows at home.

Over the next hour Hugh tells me more about Dorothy and I make notes. I interrupt at certain points, asking him to clarify. The detail is vital.

'Dorothy grew up in Tamarisk Bay,' he explains, 'at least that's where she was living before the war. She was born in East Anglia, but then the family moved down south for health reasons. She had a brother, a few years younger than her. She always spoke fondly of him, his name was Kenneth as I recall. I think she felt bad about leaving him behind when she joined the land army, but in wartime we all had to make difficult decisions.'

'And you think she might have returned here, to her hometown?'

'I imagine so, yes.'

'But you didn't keep in touch?'

'War disrupts lives, divides families. You're young, it's hard for you to understand.'

As I listen to Hugh, I sense a murkiness in between the lines of his story. I'm wading through muddy waters, with a sludge of unspoken truths slowing my progress.

He glances at his watch. 'It's coming up to 8pm, they'll be closing soon.'

The waitress comes over to our table and clears away the cups, which are still half full. A couple of other tables also need cleaning and then she brings out a broom and starts putting chairs on tables before sweeping.

'Must be our cue to leave,' I say. 'Just one more question. What makes you think that Dorothy is in danger? And a photo, do you have any photos of her?'

'That's two things,' he says.

I smile. He puts his hand inside his blazer and takes out a small black and white photo. The woman in the photo is about my age, maybe a year or two younger. Her hair is plaited and wound around her head. She's wearing corduroy trousers and a thick jumper, with a scarf wrapped around her neck.

'Of course, this was twenty-five years ago. And the answer to your other question, well, I'll explain more if you decide to take on the case.'

'Hugh, I'll work through all you have told me and I'll have a think. I don't know if I can help, to be honest with you. But if I can, I will. Where can I find you, if and when I have any information?'

He writes his address down on a slip of paper from his pocketbook.

'I'm in temporary lodgings, for the moment. Mrs Summer is the landlady. She'll take a message if I'm not there when you call.'

'Won't she wonder who I am?'

'You can say you're my niece, if you like, if it will make things easier. Mrs Juke, there's one other thing. We haven't spoken about money.'

I raise an eyebrow. At no stage in our conversation had I thought that my skills at detecting had any financial value. But now I stop to think about it, it makes sense. He is employing me to do a job. I have no idea what the going rate might be. Enough to buy a five-star pram for Bean, rather than a bargain basement one? Enough to treat Greg to a new set of darts, or a season ticket to Brighton Football Club? Maybe enough to repay the loan dad gave us for our car?

'There'll be out-of-pocket expenses too, bus fares, taxi fares,' Hugh says.

'Yes, of course. Can I work out some figures and come back to you?'

He nods, we stand and shake hands.

'What happens if I can't find her?' I say.

'I'll still pay you, for your time. But I have faith in you. I'm certain you won't let me down.'

We leave the café together and walk along the seafront. A uniformed policeman is pacing up and down close to the Pier entrance. It's not unusual to see a bobby on his beat, but once I leave Hugh to take my homeward route, I notice the policeman turn to follow Hugh. I hold back from taking the next right, which would lead me home. Instead I slow my pace and walk behind the policeman for a while. Of course, it is possible that the policeman's route coincides with Hugh's and that any mystery is entirely in my imagination. It's been a strange week, come to that, it's been a strange year and right now I have a feeling it's going to be a whole lot stranger before the year is out.

Rehearsing excuses for being even later home than I had anticipated, I realise that Hugh has stopped beside one of the seafront shelters. The policeman also appears to hesitate and then he turns and starts walking towards me. As he draws alongside me, I say, 'Good evening, officer. Could you tell me the time?' Hardly original and made even more obvious when I stuff my hands in my pockets so that he doesn't spot my wristwatch.

'A little after eight, miss,' he replies before walking on.

Greg returns home happy, having played one of his best matches since he joined the darts team.

'Pleased I persuaded you to join, after all?' I say, as we clear up after supper.

'One of your better ideas,' he says and wraps his arms around my middle. 'Bean, your father is not only good-looking, but talented into the bargain.'

'And modest?'

'Of course. And now, wife, I intend to go and spread out over the settee, and replay those brilliant shots in my mind. Did I tell you I got a bullseye? My first?'

'Er, yes, several times, I think. You go off and spread. I'll be in in time for *Z Cars* and at that point I will budge you over to make room, so enjoy it while it lasts.'

I hear him switch on the TV and I take the opportunity to read through the notes I made earlier. I've always been fascinated with the idea of land girls. Women who often knew nothing about the land, ending up as experts in planting and ploughing. The camaraderie must have been wonderful and yet it was the brutality of war that made it necessary. Good things coming from bad.

My dad fought in the war, but his time as a soldier was brief. He was barely nineteen when he joined up and a year later the war ended. He has never spoken about that time. I don't know how close he came to death, either killing or watching his friends being killed.

On my next visit to see him I raise the topic, uncertain of the response I may get. There has been a steady flow of patients and, as the last one leaves, there's time for dad to relax while I put the kettle on. Since Bean is preventing me from drinking tea, I've discovered hot water with lemon is a perfect alternative. The kettle boils and dad and Charlie come through from the treatment room.

Dad takes his usual seat at the kitchen table, with his back to the door and Charlie at his feet. I sit opposite him, in my usual place, beside the cooker. This isn't about habit or routine. Every item on the work surface has its own special place. The tea caddy is always to the left of the sugar jar, the biscuit barrel nestles on the bottom shelf of the cupboard nearest to the sink. In the sitting room the constant position of each piece of furniture has resulted in little indentations in the carpet. Every item in the house forms part of a road map for dad, to make sure he never loses his way.

'Busy day, wasn't it?' I say, as we sip our drinks.

'Good one, though. Very satisfying. Mrs Barnard doesn't need another appointment and Mr Haywood tells me he has been finding it much easier to do the stairs now that his knee has settled.'

'A marvel, that's what you are.'

'Well, thank you, princess. Although, you may be a touch biased.'

'Do you ever wonder what your life would be like if you had stayed in the police force? If you hadn't had your accident?'

'I don't find *what ifs* that helpful. It is as it is and that's fine for me. Besides, I'm getting a taste of detective work vicariously.'

'Ah, yes, well.'

'Have you taken on the new case? The chap from the library?'

'Can't get much past you, can I?'

My dad's intuition is what would have made him a brilliant detective. I hope I've inherited a little of it.

'Before you say anything about Bean, or Greg for that matter, don't worry,' I say. 'I'm not going to be racing about all over the place. If I take it on, and I haven't given him a definite answer yet, then I plan to enlist help.'

'Staff?' he says, smiling.

'Poirot uses his sidekick Hastings to dig around for clues. It's surprising what you can find out just by talking to people. In fact, I thought I'd start with you.'

'You're not going to ask me to breach patient confidentiality, are you?'

'Nothing like that. But what I'd like to ask you may make you feel uncomfortable.'

He looks quizzical and I wonder what possibilities he's playing around with in his mind.

'Will you tell me about your time in the army, about the war?'

'Oh, I didn't see that coming.'

'No pun intended?' My dad and I don't shy away from the reality of his blindness, but that doesn't stop us from laughing about it now and then. 'Seriously though, are you able to give me a sense of how things were back then? I can imagine a lot of it, but I want to discard assumptions and focus on facts.'

'I'm impressed, you've been listening to my advice, after all.'

'Of course.'

'It was a time of contradictions,' he pauses, as if he is trying to shuffle his memories into a semblance of order. 'Many terrible moments, interspersed with bright ones. I made new friends and lost others. There was a shift in priorities, suddenly all the things we thought were important before the war, became insignificant.'

'Kind of like when you lost your sight?'

'In some respects, yes. Our focus was on staying alive and keeping those around us safe from harm.'

'Did you know who to trust?'

'Interesting question. In the main, yes. We soon learned the importance of respect, and how critical it was to follow orders. When your commanding officer tells you to do something, you can't afford to question his reasons, you need to act.'

'But what if he's wrong? There must have been errors of judgement?'

'Yes, I'm sure there were. But I was lucky, my platoon was responsible for moving goods.'

'You didn't have to fight?'

'Every day was a fight. Making sure our convoys reached their destination without incident. One day I watched the truck in front of mine being blown to smithereens. Nothing left of the truck, the goods, or the soldiers.'

'You must have been terrified. You were so young. Five years younger than I am now. Didn't you want to run away?'

'That's what I mean about contradictions. There was such a sense of togetherness. You knew that your actions weren't only helping your fellow soldiers, but all the people back home, a whole nation. Running away would mean letting everyone down.'

'Do you think it changed you? The terrible things you saw, living with fear every day.'

'What doesn't kill you makes you stronger. That's what they say, isn't it?'

'Thanks dad.'

'What for?'

'For explaining, for talking about it. I appreciate it's hard, stirring up memories you'd rather forget.'

'Will it help with your new investigation?'

'Yes, I think it will.'

'Are you going to tell me about it?'

'I will, but not yet. I need to get it straight in my mind first. Like I said before, I've been asked to track down a woman, but I'm still not sure why.'

'Why the person is missing?'

'No, I mean, why me?'

'Well, perhaps what you did for Zara has gained you a reputation?'

'I could take that one of two ways,' I say, smiling. 'Anyway, time for me to get home and sort out supper.'

'Don't let this search come between you. You and Greg. Your new baby and your husband need to be your priorities.'

'It's okay, dad, I have it in hand.'

The truth is, I don't.

Chapter 5

They don't know it yet, but Phyllis and Libby Frobisher are about to be enlisted into the Janie Juke mystery-solving team.

Phyllis was my English teacher at grammar school and is best described as the grandmother I wished for, but never had. Phyllis's cottage is a perfect complement to her character; neat, thoughtfully decorated and not showy. Lavender Cottage nestles in the heart of Tidehaven Old Town. To reach the cottage you need to wind your way down an alley, which is too narrow for a car to pass through. As a result, I have a sense of being back in Tudor times when the cottage was built and when the favoured mode of transport was a horse and cart and good old-fashioned, *Shanks's pony*.

In line with its name, either side of the front door stand two large stone pots, planted with English lavender. It's late in the season now, but even in its autumnal state, as the flower stems are brushed by the wind they give off a delicate sweet scent.

Pushing open the wooden gate, I step onto the footpath and spy a ball of ginger fluff, partly hidden by a hydrangea bush that sits under the bay window. For a moment it's as though it is part of the bush itself, the heavy flowers tinged bronze with autumn. But then the tail appears and with a flash the cat crosses the path and disappears into the hedge.

'A new member of the household?' I say, when Phyllis appears. The last time Phyllis was in the library, I mentioned I might call in, so I'm not surprised when she opens the door before I have time to use the quaint brass pixie knocker.

'No, she belongs next door, but appears to prefer my milk. I shouldn't have started it I suppose, but there was one cold morning when she sat on my doorstep looking so forlorn. Ever since, she kicks up such a fuss if the saucer isn't down and well filled.'

'You're too soft.'

'Yes, I probably am. Come on in, kettle's on and I've made flapjack. Bean okay with flapjack?'

'Flapjack is perfect. Can I take a quick peek at your back garden? I haven't seen it since you had the new patio laid.'

'Feel free,' she says, opening the back door. 'I won't come out, I'm in my slippers, but go and have a wander. If you walk to the end of the garden and look back at the cottage, you'll get the best view.'

'It's perfect,' I say, returning a few minutes later. 'It's got me thinking about our scruffy patch of lawn. Will you help me with some ideas to spruce it up? Greg and I are hopeless, we barely know the difference between a flower and a weed. It would be brilliant for Bean to have a proper garden to run around in, instead of the tip it is at the moment.'

'If it's ideas you want, no problem. I can't promise to do much digging though. There was a time when I'd have a go at most things, but the best I can do now is supervise. Let's go through to the sitting room, it's cosier in there. Then you can tell me the real reason you're here.'

There's not much I can get past Phyllis. She's as intuitive as dad and knows me almost as well. The pretext for my visit was to get her opinion on the latest Agatha Christie, but I didn't expect her to fall for that rather feeble excuse. The library van is where we talk about books.

'How is Greg?' she says.

I smile.

'Does he know you're about to embark on another case?'

Phyllis may be my stalwart supporter in many aspects of my life, but she disapproved of me getting so involved with the search for Zara. It's unlikely she will be any more encouraging this time around, particularly as Bean's arrival is creeping ever closer.

'I have a plan,' I say.

'Ah.'

'I'm going to enlist help. In fact, that's why I'm here.'

She stands up and goes to the window that looks out onto a large beech tree, which takes up one corner of the back garden. Its leaves have turned a deep caramel colour and a brisk wind is blowing through the branches, making them dip and sway.

'How are the hiccups?' she says.

'Your lavender is very calming. Perhaps I should keep a handful in my bag, take it out as and when required.'

Aside from my difficulties with tea and various foods, I have developed a propensity for hiccups whenever I am anxious or over-excited. The arrival of hiccups in the middle of an argument, or at the point of discovering a vital clue, is less than helpful. I put my hands on my midriff and stroke it a few times. I don't want Bean to feel unloved.

I sink down into a well-worn armchair, which is close enough to the cheery coal fire for me to hear the crackles and spits as the flames flicker. Phyllis sets the tray with drinks and flapjack on a low table between us.

'Why do you think I can help you?' she says.

'It's information I'm after at the moment. How well do you remember your pupils?'

'All of them? We're talking over forty years.'

'I know. It's a lot to ask, but if I tell you all I know about a particular family, then maybe...?'

'Fire away.'

'A brother and sister. Dorothy is the girl's name and her brother was Kenneth. He was a bit younger than her and their father suffered badly with asthma and bronchitis. The family moved down here because the doctor told him it would help with his chest complaint - the sea air and all that.'

'There are several families who meet that description,' she says. 'There was an influx at one point. They all wanted to move away from the industrial cities, the smog was dreadful. I'm assuming you are talking wartime?'

'No, it would have been before the war. Dorothy was in her twenties in the war, so we're talking a few years before that. I think the family came from East Anglia originally, maybe Peterborough.'

'Surname?'

'Elm.'

She appears pensive and pours herself another cup of tea. 'More drink for you? I've left the kettle on the gas and I've plenty of lemons.'

'I'm okay, thanks. I don't expect you to have the answer straightaway. Have a think, maybe something will come to you, a memory, a flashback.'

'Nothing else you can tell me? What about the mother?'

'I'm not sure. I can try and find out. Will it help?'

'Perhaps.'

She puts her empty cup and saucer onto the tray and adds a few more coals to the fire. The mantelpiece displays a collection of delicate china thimbles and I wonder how long it must take her to dust them all.

'You mustn't worry about Greg and me,' I say, 'we're fine.'

'Sure?'

'Certain. We're just finding our way, still learning about each other.'

'Don't block him out. You'll need him when Bean arrives.'

On the bus back from Phyllis's I mull over her advice, what she said and what was left unsaid. Greg and I have reached a stage in our relationship where we are each jostling for a place, like horses at a starting gate. In the two years we've been married it's like the ground beneath us is constantly shifting. Maybe that's what married life is like. I don't have much to compare it with.

Mum walked out soon after dad's accident, when it became clear that he would be leaning on her in more ways than one. Aside from her postal address somewhere up north, I know little about the life she has chosen. My in-laws, Nell and Jimmy Juke, appear to have a traditional relationship, in that she complains a lot, but he rarely listens. They rub along together, but there seems to be little joy. Maybe the joy and passion go out of a relationship when you've been together as long as they have, or maybe there wasn't much there to start with.

Nell and Jimmy met and married straight after the war, as did mum and dad. Life and attitudes have changed. The war years showed women they could have so much more, be so much more. Now we are approaching the end of a decade that has brought us a different range of freedoms. For the first time since the war young men don't have to join up (I need to remind Greg how lucky he is) and married women can take charge when it comes to birth control (I don't need any reminding on that front).

The search for Dorothy Elm intrigues me. Not just the challenge of tracking down a missing person, if indeed she is missing. From what I've learned about her so far, she sounds like one of the new breed of women, women who broke the mould, who were prepared to try new challenges. Perhaps she and I have something in common.

I agreed with Hugh that I'd let him know my decision about the case by the weekend. I also need to work out my fee. It's not like I can ask around, I'm guessing there aren't many private investigators in Tamarisk Bay, at least none I know of. Thinking laterally, my thoughts go to Libby Frobisher. Libby, Phyllis Frobisher's favourite and only grand-daughter, has recently moved from Cornwall to land a job as a journalist with the *Tidehaven Observer*. It was Libby's article about my involvement in the search for Zara that led Hugh to come knocking, figuratively speaking.

Using Libby's wages as a benchmark for my own fees feels appropriate, after all, we are both investigating, in one way or another. It's a bit of a liberty to ask Libby straight out, but I've browsed the *Job vacancies* pages in the *Tidehaven Observer*, and even checked through a copy of the *Brighton Argus*, and am none the wiser, so it looks as though it may be my only option.

We arrange to meet in my favourite café at the bottom of London Road. *Jefferson's* is a cross between a café and a club. Richie, the owner, loves music as much as making coffee, probably more so.

'Got a scoop for me?' Libby asks, as we nestle ourselves into a corner of the café, away from the jukebox. The music is great, but sometimes it's difficult to hear anything else.

'No,' I hesitate to say anything more.

Think of the fizz that hovers over a glass of lemonade, the moment you pour it from the bottle, and that's Libby. Perhaps I'm doing her an injustice. Fizz can be amusing, but ineffectual. Libby is usually the former, but never the latter. She has become a friend, but it's the journalist in her that is on duty today, poised for that snippet of news that will lead to a front-page splash and another pat on the back from her editor.

'I'm after information from you this time,' I say, stirring sugar into my coffee. Bean is encouraging my sweet tooth, at least that's my excuse.

'Information about what? You get to hear more gossip than I do in that library of yours. Why do you think we're friends?'

I raise an eyebrow.

'Only joking,' she says.

'It's kind of personal.'

'Are we talking love life? If so, forget it. No-one on the scene at present and no-one waiting in the wings, but I live in hope.'

'Not love, work.'

'Boring.'

'It's about money, so not completely boring. Do you mind telling me how much you earn?'

'Cut to the chase, why don't you? Not after my job, are you?'

'No, nothing like that. It's just...'

'You've been asked to take on a case, haven't you? Go on, you can trust me.'

I laugh and shake my head.

'It's a fair swap. I tell you my salary, you tell me who you're working for? Go on, give me a little taster, to liven up my day. All I've got to look forward to is the annual general meeting of the Women's Institute. You should take pity on a poor reporter.'

As a junior reporter Libby is still on a junior's wage. Nevertheless, the thought of those few extra pounds is enticing. I decide to ask Hugh for an hourly rate, based on half of Libby's, as I figure I'm still learning. My next dilemma is how to calculate the number of hours I spend working on the case. Can I charge for the time I'm tending the library and mulling over clues? It's clear that this private detective work is not straightforward.

I needn't have worried. Hugh clearly has more money than sense and offers me a lump sum, which far exceeds anything I could have hoped for. Half now and half at the end of my search.

'And if I don't find Dorothy?' I ask him, during our next meeting in Tensing Gardens.

'I'm confident you will find her, but I'll pay you regardless, plus any out-of-pocket expenses.'

'How long have I got? When will we call a halt?'

He glances down at my midriff and smiles. 'I think you'll be the judge of that, or your baby will.'

He holds out his hand. 'Shake on it?'

There's a rush of exhilaration as we shake. I'm embarking on a new career. I stumbled into my search for Zara, but this one will be different and it's not just because I'm being paid.

Chapter 6

As Bean grows, my regular visits to the ante-natal clinic provide me with reassurance that all is well. Several of the mums who go along to Briarsbank Maternity Home are now familiar faces, but only for the odd hello and a few words. But my friendship with Nikki Bright is more than that. Most weeks, after the ante-natal clinic, we walk for a while and shelter in a café if the weather is bad, or sit in the park, if there's sunshine to be had.

Today is the kind of October day that is trying to disguise itself as summer. Leaves have turned trees into kaleidoscopes of colour that would make any artist envious. But there is little warmth in the sun, so we stop at a favourite café and order hot drinks.

'Can you feel them both kicking?' I ask her. 'I mean, do they move at the same time, or is it just a jumble of arms and legs?'

She smiles and takes my hand, placing it gently on her midriff. I'm struggling with all that one little Bean is doing to my body, I have no idea how she is managing with twins.

'They're on the go all the time, if it's not one it's the other. Goodness knows what it'll be like once they're here. I won't have a minute to breathe. How about Bean? Is it a fidget?'

'Mostly after I've eaten.'

'And the hiccups? Are they still a problem?'

'When I'm anxious, or over-excited. I should have asked the midwife about it.'

'Next time, maybe? Anyway, I wanted to run something past you,' she says, pushing her empty cup away and relaxing back in the chair. 'I'm thinking of having a dinner party. It's a chance to meet a few new people. I haven't made many friends since we arrived. Well, just you, really.

Frank's got all his work colleagues, of course, but there's only so much police talk I can handle.'

When Frank Bright got the job as Detective Sergeant at Tidehaven Police Station it meant uprooting and moving house, leaving Nikki's parents and in-laws back up north, and her in need of a new support network.

'I know what you mean about shop talk, I'm forever having to listen to the intricacies of building projects and it's starting to get on my nerves.' I take a teaspoon and stir my coffee, even though I haven't added any sugar. 'Nikki, can I just say, I'm pleased we have stayed friends, after all that business with Zara. I realise it must have been difficult for you being caught in the middle.'

'I'll admit I struggled for a while. Frank will always be my first priority, but friends are important too. So, what do you think about the dinner party idea? I'd like you and Greg to come too.'

'Sounds like fun, but it'll be a lot of work for you, won't it? Are you sure it won't be too much?'

Greg is none too keen. I remind him of the occasions when I've sat on the sidelines while he's been planning strategy with the darts team, or describing the latest Brighton football match to dad, kick by kick.

'Won't the detective think it's strange, you turning up at his house?'

'He knows Nikki and I are friends. At least I'm pretty sure he does. If not, he'll have a pleasant surprise. They live on the Goldhill Estate, in one of the new houses. You can consider it research, for when you build ours.'

Since Greg took on the building apprenticeship at Mowbray and Son, I've been teasing him that one day he can build us our own home. It may be a while off, but I'm prepared to wait.

When the evening of the dinner party arrives, I take extra care with my make-up and wear my favourite purple smock dress. The long, lean line of current fashion is clearly not for me at present and will have to wait until after Bean's arrival. But I can still have fun with my hair. I take three scarves from my wardrobe, one purple, one white and the third one a mix of the two. I weave them into a tight plait and wind the result around my head, tucking my unruly waves behind my ears, leaving my fringe loose.

'You're a bit of a dish,' I tell Greg, as he checks his hair in the hall mirror. 'Good job I married you.'

'Ditto,' he says.

'The dish, or the marriage?'

'Both. And stylish headband, by the way. Do we need to take anything?'

'I bought a box of *Milk Tray*. Everyone loves chocolate.'

'Didn't you say the only thing Nikki can stomach is chips with loads of salt and vinegar?'

'Well, you'll be happy then, won't you?' I say, poking him in the ribs.

'Watch it, or I'll tickle you and Bean will be performing somersaults. Kiss for your husband before we go?'

'Of course.' I lean into him and press my cheek against his.

'Let's get a dog,' he says. My hair has fallen down in front of his face, making his voice muffled.

'Did you just say what I think you said? A dog? Where did that idea come from?'

'I'm serious. I can take him to work with me on the days you're in the library. A couple of the lads have dogs, he'd have company. You could take him to your dad's on Tuesdays and Thursdays and Charlie could teach him manners. It'll be brilliant.'

He has it all worked out.

'Don't you think we should wait until Bean arrives? So we get used to being a threesome before we add a puppy into the mix?'

'We don't need to get a puppy, we could get an older dog, rehome one. Think about it at least.'

Frank and Nikki's semi-detached house is modern and stylish, with matching furnishings. The curtains match the wallpaper and the cushions match the sofa. Perfect for a magazine photo, but soulless. Give me my quirky little terraced house any day.

They both meet us at the door and we follow them through the entrance hall, which leads into a long, narrow living room, set out with a lounge at one end and a dining room at the other. Nikki must have spent hours preparing the table, which is set for eight people. Cutlery shines and starched napkins are folded into a fan shape and tucked into gleaming crystal glasses.

Frank takes our coats and organises drinks. It is strange to see him in his off-duty setting. I half expect him to take me to one side and quiz me about Zara. The case has yet to reach the courts and I am uncomfortably aware that at some point I will be seeing him in very different circumstances - the inside of a court room, to be precise.

But for now, he is all smiles, as is Nikki, who shows us to our places around the table. She encourages everyone to help themselves to the fascinating arrangement of cheese and pineapple cubes, skewered and stuck into a grapefruit. Each couple is divided, so that we are all sitting next to a new acquaintance. She appears to be in total command of the social setting, as though she has done it for years. So different from the timid mother-to-be I first met a few months ago.

Greg is sitting opposite me and I catch snippets of his conversation as he chats to one of Nikki's neighbours. The woman, introduced to us as Marjorie, is older than us, in her early forties perhaps, with a pinched look about her. By contrast, her husband, Patrick, has an open countenance and a booming voice. His laugh, which I hear frequently throughout the meal, is a deep-throated chuckle that is contagious. Each time I hear it I can't help but smile.

My supper companions are Joanne and Howard. They are both chatterboxes and I wonder whether their teenage children are the same, which must result in extremely noisy meal-times at their house, or perhaps the kids don't even try to compete. Our conversation topics range from sport (mainly football), the weather, and plans for Guy Fawkes, which is only weeks away. Like all well-behaved supper guests, the trickier subjects of religion and politics are carefully avoided.

'The kids keep pushing for us to take the boat out,' Joanne says.

'You've got a yacht?' I say, trying not to sound too impressed.

'Oh no, nothing quite so fancy,' Howard says, 'just a little fishing boat. It was my dad's. I spent all my summer holidays in that boat, either on the water, or sprucing it up. But my two are hopeless, they're up for it when there's fun to be had, but when it comes to anything that requires a bit of elbow grease they're nowhere to be seen.'

All this talk of fishing boats makes me think of Hugh and Dorothy.

'You're looking pensive,' Joanne says, passing me the gravy. 'You run the mobile library, don't you? I haven't been to the library for years. Last time I called in was when the kids were tiny. Phyllis Frobisher ran it back then. I always felt I might get told off if I chose the wrong book.

"*Think of your reading as food for the mind.*" That was her mantra when I was at school.'

'She taught you English?'

'Yes, she must have taught half of Tamarisk Bay.'

'You grew up around here?'

Joanne nods and casts me an enquiring glance.

'You don't happen to know the Elm family, do you? Dorothy and Kenneth - brother and sister.'

'The surname seems familiar, but I can't think why. Are they friends of yours?'

'No, nothing like that. It's just that a friend of a friend is trying to get back in touch with them.'

She reaches behind me and taps Howard on the arm. 'Howie, do you know a chap called Kenneth Elm?'

'Do you mean the vet?'

'Oh, now I remember,' she says, 'it was Mr Elm who cared for Flash when she got cat flu. Pleasant chap.'

For a moment I feel like hugging Howard in gratitude for giving me my first kernel of information. Instead, I smile and pass him the horseradish.

The dinner is more expertly cooked and presented than any roast I've ever had a hand in. I'm expecting Greg to rave about the Yorkshires for weeks to come. With dessert polished off we're invited to adjourn into the lounge end of the room, with the offer of coffee and mints.

Throughout the meal Nikki bobs in and out of the kitchen, clearing away plates and bringing in fresh ones. Frank is at the far end of the table, talking with one of the neighbours. I catch the odd snippet of their conversation, which seems to be focused on the problems on the estate. 'Hoodlums' and 'vandalism' are mentioned, until Nikki casts a disapproving sideways glance in her husband's direction.

With all her fetching and carrying, I notice that Nikki has barely had time to eat anything. With no offers of help coming from her husband, or from any of the other guests, I extricate myself from Howard, as he is about to regale me with his memories of a childhood bonfire that ended in disaster.

'Let me help,' I say and gather up some of the dishes.

'No, you sit still, I'm fine,' Nikki says.

I take no notice of her and follow her out to the kitchen, laden with crockery.

'You look done in. I'll sort the teas and coffees out, you sit down for a bit.'

'No, you're a guest.'

'And you're expecting twins. If you won't let me help, then ask Frank.'

'He doesn't like being seen to do women's work in front of other people.'

'I hope you're kidding. Those ideas went out years ago.'

'I'm not into all that social revolution nonsense. Besides, Frank is older than me, he's had different experiences. He remembers the war. He was only a boy, but his memories are still vivid.' She is speaking in hushed tones, a frown appearing on her face.

'Then he should remember what women achieved back then, his mum probably helped with the war effort, all the women did.'

'All I'm saying is I'm happy with Frank as he is. He works hard and he's kind and loving. It hasn't been easy for him you know, losing his first wife like that.' Nikki's face is flushed and her bottom lip trembles as she continues. 'Did you know about Lois?'

'Lois?'

'His first wife. She died very young. They'd only been married a short while. He was in a mess when I first met him.'

She pulls out a handkerchief that was tucked inside the sleeve of her bolero and dabs her eyes.

'I'm really sorry,' I say, 'I didn't mean to upset you.'

'Take no notice of me, it's these babies. They take over your body and leave you an emotional mess. I'm sure it'll be easier once they've arrived.' She takes my arm and leads me out into the hall. 'There's a photo of her.'

The black and white photo is framed and hanging over a small hall table. On the table is a vase of fresh carnations.

'We keep her memory alive. She was part of his life, so it's the right thing to do. I think it speaks volumes about the kind of man he is, deep down.'

Lois was a beauty, dark haired, trim figure and stylishly dressed. In the photo she looks around the same age as Nikki and yet there is more of a worldliness about her.

'How did you meet Frank?' I say.

'In the supermarket, believe it or not. He looked so forlorn. Lois had been gone two years and he still looked like a lost soul.'

'Well, good for you. I'm happy that it has all worked out for you both.'

'Are you two going to be joining us any time soon?' Frank's commanding voice startles me. I struggle to think of him as a lost soul, shopping for single portions, but it's a reminder to me of dad's mantra not to make assumptions about people.

'Think of each individual you meet as a diamond with many cut edges,' dad has told me on more than one occasion.

'And flaws?'

'Always.'

Nikki leaves the kitchen, carrying a wooden board displaying an arrangement of cheese and biscuits. I thought we'd moved onto coffee and mints, but it would seem I'm ahead of myself. Frank and I hover in the hallway, in front of the photo of Lois.

'She was very beautiful,' I say, 'I hadn't realised...'

He gazes at the photo, then removes a wilted carnation petal from the hall table. 'Delicate flowers are lovely, until they die,' he says and shakes his head as if he is trying to clear away painful memories. 'How are you, Mrs Juke?'

'Very well, thank you. But Janie, please.'

'Settling back into married life? And the library? What will they do without you when you have your baby?'

'Oh, we'll sort something out. I don't want to give up work, I like what I do.'

'Was that a casual conversation you were having earlier, with Howard and Joanne, or are you following a line of enquiry? Is there something you need to talk to me about?'

I have a brief flashback to that night at the Pier Café and the policeman who seemed to be taking more than a passing interest in Hugh. I hesitate for a moment, sorely tempted to ask his advice.

'Work and motherhood don't mix, not in my opinion,' he says. 'But then, I'm old-fashioned, or so my wife tells me.'

'And you have twins on the way, that's exciting.'

He smiles and nods and we move through to join the others. For the rest of the evening the conversations pass me by. All I can think about is Hugh. I have my first lead now that I know where to find Kenneth Elm. But for all my questioning and all his explaining, there is still one vital piece of information that Hugh has omitted to tell me. Dorothy is in danger and I need to know why.

Chapter 7

I've been to *Crossland Vets* a couple of times with dad and Charlie, but I tend to stay in the waiting area and let dad go in. So, I've never chatted to any of the vets. Charlie is due for his annual booster jab, which provides me with the perfect opportunity to gather my first piece of evidence.

When I telephone to make the appointment, the receptionist informs me I will be seeing the duty vet, so all I can do is keep my fingers crossed. When Charlie and I arrive for the appointment I glance up at the names listed on the board and there he is, Dorothy's brother, Mr Kenneth Elm. He's been here all along.

'Who will I be seeing?' I ask the receptionist.

'Mr Carruthers is the duty vet today.'

'Great, thanks. And Mr Elm?'

'Mr Elm?'

'Yes, er, is he on duty today?'

'Your appointment is with the duty vet. Is Charlie one of Mr Elm's patients?'

It's clear that the requirements for a vet's receptionist are not dissimilar to a doctor's, that is, an ability to protect the professionals from time-wasters. After a short wait we are called through by a man who could easily take seasonal work as Father Christmas. His beard is so white and fluffy I have the strangest desire to tug at it to make sure it's real.

'Good morning, I'm Mr Carruthers,' he says, indicating to me that he would like Charlie up on the examining table. 'Ah, I think we're going to struggle,' he says, looking at my midriff.

'Not sure I've ever been able to lift him, but at present, no, definitely not.'

'Don't worry, it's Charlie, is that right?'

I acknowledge him and then hold Charlie still as the injection goes into his rump. Charlie grumbles a little, but a couple of biscuits later and any discomfort is a distant memory.

We are about to leave when I remember the other reason for my visit.

'Can I ask your advice?' I say.

'About Charlie?'

'No, something else. My husband has suggested we get a dog.'

'Another one?'

'No, Charlie is dad's dog.'

'Yes, yes, of course,' he says, fiddling with some packets on a shelving unit behind him. I wonder what I need to do to gain his full attention.

'I'm having a baby,' I say, holding my hands over my midriff. The ruse works as he turns away from the shelving unit that has been pre-occupying him and faces me.

'My husband has suggested we get a dog,' I repeat. 'And I'm wondering if you have any advice?'

His eyes narrow, suggesting he is struggling to understand me. On this occasion we are clearly not sharing a common language, even though we both speak English.

'Baby, then dog, or dog, then baby - is there a recommended order of events from your experience?' I say.

'Oh, I see, yes, of course. I'm sorry, Mrs Juke, but I don't have any advice to give you. There are so many factors to consider, for example, your daily routine. How will you manage if you have a baby with gripe and a mischievous puppy? Then there's your husband to care for, meals to prepare, housework and so on.'

'Yes,' I say, 'well, thank you, I've taken up enough of your time. Come on, Charlie, we must head home to our domestic chores.'

There is no point in trying to explain to the delightful Mr Carruthers how far removed my life is from the one he imagines.

A few days later and I am with Charlie again, but in a different place entirely. All the chatter from Howard and Joanne about their fishing boat, coming so soon after Hugh's wartime recollections, inspired me to make a wild suggestion to dad. Dad's passion has always been the sea and anything that lives in or near it, but since he lost his sight, fishing expeditions haven't exactly featured on the to-do list. But when Howard and Joanne said they were more than happy to loan me the boat for the day, it seemed like too good a chance to miss. I'll admit it was one of my crazier ideas and I was surprised when dad agreed.

I have managed to get all of us into the boat without falling into the water, which in itself is a minor miracle. As I release the rope and push us away from the quayside I'll admit to having a flutter of misgivings.

'Here we are then, a blind man, his pregnant daughter and a dog who appears to be scared of water,' dad says, as he holds himself as still as possible, while the sea moves all around us. 'Add to that, the fact we have chosen to have this adventure in the winter.'

'No, it's still autumn, winter doesn't officially start until the 1st of December. I don't know why I didn't think about this years ago, although I suspect access to a boat was the biggest hurdle to overcome,' I say confidently.

'I can think of bigger hurdles,' he says, smiling. 'The biggest one at the moment is the noise Charlie is making.

I've never heard him whine like that. Are you sure he hasn't trodden on a splinter?'

'He's just being a scaredy-cat - or dog.'

Dad is right. The weather isn't ideal and I'll admit I hadn't checked the forecast. But I've made a flask of coffee and we're both well wrapped up.

'We don't have to be out for long and we're not going far. I'll get us away from the shore, then I'll drop the anchor and we'll be well protected in this little harbour. Let's get a taste for it and then we can do it again, maybe on a calmer day.'

My image of dad and I relaxing, as the boat bobbed along, with a fishing line trailing in the water and Charlie stretched out at our feet, turns out to be just that - an image. I failed to realise I know nothing about fixing the bait, or casting the line. Dad talks me through it, but all I succeed in doing is getting the line in a tangle and spilling the box of bait into the bottom of the boat. Charlie immediately seizes the opportunity to have an early lunch.

'No, Charlie, it's nasty, leave it,' I shout. But he already has a mouthful of the bait and looks vaguely pleased with himself. 'Oh, jeepers, this is turning out to be a farce of immense proportions. All that needs to happen now is for one of us to fall into the sea and we will have had the perfect day.'

Dad and I dissolve into laughter at the same moment and soon I am hiccuping in-between the giggles, which makes me laugh even more.

'Stop, I can't get my breath,' I say, with tears running down my face, merging with the salt spray blown up by the wind.

'I thought you got hiccups when you were anxious.'

'Yes, well...' I can't say any more as the hiccups have taken over completely. I go to stand up, thinking that movement may help to settle Bean's protestations. This is the point Charlie decides to be sick.

'Oh no,' I say, as this final catastrophe confirms this to be a memorable day. Memorable for all the wrong reasons.

'Is he alright, Janie?'

'Er, well, he's got rid of the bait, so better out than in. But he's looking decidedly peaky.'

Charlie is now crouching down beside dad's feet, moaning gently and looking forlorn.

'It can't be too harmful, or we'd be poisoning the fish, rather than catching them. But I think a quick trip to the vet when we're back on shore might be best,' dad says.

My second visit to the vet in the same week is fortuitous, or would have been if it resulted in me meeting the elusive Mr Elm. But, as I've come to discover, life is anything but perfect. Although, on some days, it gets close to it.

I turn up with Charlie at the open surgery session. No appointment needed, just a lot of patience. There are two rabbits, a kitten and a guinea pig in front of us in the queue, with an elderly St Bernard paying his bill, or rather his owner is.

The noticeboard above the reception desk announces the two duty vets, Mr Carruthers and Mr Elm. It will be first-come, first-served, so all I can do, once again, is keep my fingers crossed. The owner of the kitten sits beside me, putting the cat basket on the floor beside Charlie.

'I'm impressed, your dog is so well behaved,' she says.

'He has his moments.'

'Most dogs growl at Chintzy, scare her half to death.'

'I'm sure she'll get her own back when she's older.'

'No, she's so timid. She won't even go into the garden at night on her own. I have to go out there with her.'

'Pets, eh,' I say, for want of a better reply. 'Charlie likes cats, I'm not sure he realises he's not supposed to. In fact, he likes all animals. He was intrigued by the hedgehog we found in the garden, until he got a bit too close and ended up with a sore nose.'

She laughs and pats Charlie's head, at which point Chintzy starts miaowing.

'Jealousy?' I say.

'Mrs Baker, can you bring Chintzy through now please.' One of the vets appears and the kitten and its owner follow him into the surgery. Seconds later Charlie and I are called through by the Father Christmas look-alike.

'And what has Charlie been up to?' Mr Carruthers asks.

'We took him fishing and he didn't realise the bait was for the fish.'

'Has he been sick?'

'A couple of times.'

'Has he eaten anything since the bait?'

'No, he's drunk a lot of water though, he seems to have an incredible thirst.'

'Well, that's no bad thing. Flush it all through, so to speak.'

The vet spends some time poking and prodding around Charlie's abdomen, then listens to his heart.

'None the worse for the experience. I think he'll be fine. He probably got rid of it all when he was sick. No harm done, just a bit rich for his digestion. You did the right thing to bring him in though. Keep an eye on him for the next twenty-four hours and if you're worried at all, bring him back.'

Having paid the bill, I stop at one of the bus shelters, sit down and take out my notebook. When Mr Elm took the delightful Chintzy through to the treatment room, I got enough of a look to be able to recognise him again, so I make a few reminder notes.

Black hair, cut short, bushy eyebrows. Dark-rimmed glasses. Angular face with a protruding chin and deep-set eyes. Height, maybe six feet, average build, rounded shoulders. In his forties?

I return Charlie to dad and report on the vet's findings.

'Not sure if I'll find it that easy to keep an eye on him,' dad says, smiling.

'He'll let you know if he's not right. You two are so in sync. Might give fishing a miss for a while though.'

'That's the best thing you've said all day.'

The next morning, when I arrive at the Central Library car park to pick up the van, I expect Hugh Furness to be waiting for me. Instead, Libby is pacing up and down in front of the van, checking her watch every few seconds.

'Oh, you're here at last,' she says.

'I'm not late, am I? What's the panic?'

'Nothing, it's just I'll be late myself unless I run. I had to see you though, to tell you about my brainwave.'

'Which brainwave would that be?'

'I've had a brilliant idea about how to flush your mysterious lady out from wherever she's hiding.'

'You have?'

'Well, it might not flush her out, but I bet you'll get some clues to take you closer to finding her. I can't explain it all now. Meet me in *Jefferson's* lunchtime?'

'I don't usually stop for lunch.'

'Twenty minutes, that's all I need.'

'Okay, see you there. Now run, or you'll be demoted.'

The morning drags, despite the van being quite busy with customers. A variety of guesses turn over in my mind as to what Libby's grand plan might be. If her brainwave involves the *Tidehaven Observer* we need to be careful. Hugh has mentioned that Dorothy could be in danger and the last thing I'd want to do is to make her location public, if that results in the wrong people finding her. The trouble is, at the moment I don't know who the wrong people are.

Lunchtime finally arrives. I encourage the last of my morning customers to leave before locking up and sticking a handwritten note on the door.

Out for lunch, back at 1.30pm

I walk as quickly as Bean will allow, taking all the short cuts and arrive at *Jefferson's* to find Libby already sitting at a table in the window.

Tamarisk Bay is neither a village or a large town, but something in between. Having lived here my whole life I used to take so much of it for granted. Now, with keen observation my watchword, I test myself each time I walk down a familiar street. When new residents make changes to a front garden, or a delivery van is parked up in a spot reserved for the local taxi, I make a mental note. Criss-crossing in-between the roads are footpaths and alleyways, perfect short cuts for locals, away from the traffic. The delicate pink fronds of the tamarisk bushes that give the town its name, separate the footpaths from people's back gardens, providing an element of privacy. As we move into autumn many of the bushes have been hammered by the wind that whips through the alleyways. It will be spring before we see the fresh new shoots emerging and by then I plan to be pushing Bean down the paths, in a pristine new pram.

'Come on, out with it,' I say, once we both have a coffee in front of us.

'Your new case involves tracking down a woman, right?'

'Yes,' I say, hoping she will detect the caution in my voice.

'And this Hugh Furness chap, he knew her in the war.'

'That's what he said, yes.'

'Well, I was thinking the newspaper could do a nostalgia feature. Remembrance Sunday is coming up, isn't it? My editor will love the idea, he's really into local history. We'd announce it in advance and ask people to write in with their anecdotes about life during wartime, good and bad.'

'Good and bad?'

'Well, life wasn't all gloom and doom. Gran says the war brought people together, it was all for one and one for all.'

'You'll be singing a Vera Lynn song next.'

'Am I brilliant or what?'

'Brilliant, yes. Just a couple of little things.'

'Don't go all practical on me and throw cold water on the idea.'

'We have to assume Dorothy doesn't want to be found, so why would she write in? We could end up with a wonderful double-page spread about wartime in Tamarisk Bay and be no closer to finding her.'

'I know, I've thought of that. But every person who does write in will be a new contact for you. These are all people who might know Dorothy, they would be her peers. You might be able to elicit some little snippet of information. Isn't that what Poirot does, focus on the detail?'

'I'll take a bet you've never read an Agatha Christie novel in your life.'

'It's an educated guess. Anyway, we've got nothing to lose. But in the meantime, you need to pin Hugh down and find out more about this apparent danger Dorothy is in. How does he know about it? He must have been in touch with her recently, mustn't he? In which case, he must have some means of contacting her. Have you asked him?'

'I know, I've thought the same thing.'

'It's like he's only telling you half the story. You need to be a bit firmer with him, Janie. I'll have a go, if you like? You're lucky, you know, having an investigative journalist on your team.'

'Let me try first and if I can't get him to open up, I'll let you loose on him, but remember not to bully the poor man.'

'I can't wait,' she says and winks.

Chapter 8

The next time I see Hugh I'm ready to interrogate him. But before I can say anything he holds a hand up as if to silence me.

'I'm being followed,' he says, launching into a fit of coughing, his eyes are cloudy, his face pale. I wait to speak until he has stopped coughing and caught his breath.

'Are you certain?'

'It's been several days now. Each evening I walk from my lodgings, down to the seafront. I like to stretch my legs after tea, take in the sea air.'

I nod, waiting for him to continue.

'The first time it happened I thought nothing of it. I guessed it was someone choosing the same route as me. But on the second evening, when I came out of my lodgings, I noticed the same man. He was standing on the other side of the road, looking towards the guest house. As soon as I emerged he turned away and lit a cigarette.'

All Hugh has told me so far leaves me thinking he is a touch paranoid.

'I decided to alter my route,' he continues, 'and when I could I paused and turned to see if he was still behind me. Sure enough, there he was.'

'Can you describe him? He's not a policeman, is he?'

'No, why do you say that?'

'No reason. So what does he look like?'

'He's about my height, wears a dark raincoat, no hat.'

'What about his face, did you see his face?'

'He was quite a way off, so I can't describe his features, but he is clean shaven and wears glasses. Dark-rimmed glasses. Why is he following me? What's his intention?'

'I can't imagine. Are you sure it's not just a coincidence? Lots of people like to walk in the evening. He might not be following you at all. Is his demeanour threatening in any way?'

'He knows I've seen him. For a couple of nights I stayed in, I thought he might get tired of waiting and give up. But then, the next time I went out, there he was.'

'I can see it must be disconcerting for you. Leave it with me. You carry on doing the same thing, don't change your routine. I have an idea.'

If my plan pays off, Hugh will have more than one follower.

'I might go out myself tonight,' I tell Greg over supper.

'Round your dad's?'

'No, I might meet up with Libby, she's at a loose end.'

'Not definite?'

'She's calling round after she's seen Phyllis, but I'm not sure what time. Then we might go for a drive. I'm guessing you'll walk round to the pub for your darts match?'

'That's fine, but if you take the car make sure you concentrate on the driving, I know what you two are like once you get chatting.'

'Have a nice time, Janie,' I say, pointedly.

'Yes, have a nice time, but be careful.'

'Three days a week I drive a 7.5 ton van around, so I think I can manage a Morris Minor, don't you?'

Libby arrives shortly after Greg's departure and as soon as we are in the car she grabs my arm. 'Exciting news, my editor says, as long as I'm the one to trawl through the letters, we can have the nostalgia feature. Oh, and the sorting needs to be done in my own time. He's expecting there to be a deluge, I think.'

'That's perfect. I'll help.'

'We can see if there's anything relevant to the case that might not be suitable for newspaper articles, if you get my drift?'

'You mean we can get to the writer before anyone else?'

'Exactly.'

It's already dark as we drive off, with the sun setting soon after 6pm. With no daylight, observations will be trickier. It also means we may not be able to use my Instamatic, as the flash will draw unwanted attention to our presence.

We drive to the end of First Avenue and park up in a lay-by. From our parked position we can easily see the doorway to Hugh's lodgings, as well as anyone loitering in the road. A few feet from the lay-by and opposite the guesthouse is a bus shelter. The shelter is closed in with wooden panelling at both ends, so it's impossible to see if anyone is inside, unless we get out of the car. However, I can see someone's legs stretched out towards the kerb.

After a few minutes, the door to the lodgings opens and Hugh steps out. He glances up and down the street, then turns right and starts to walk slowly in the direction of the seafront. A few moments later, the person who has been sitting in the bus shelter gets up and starts to follow Hugh. Now that he is in full view, I can see he's tall, slightly stooping and wearing a mac. But from where we are parked, that's all I can see.

'Now what?' Libby says.

'Let's wait a while, then we'll drive slowly in the same direction.'

'But we can't see his face, we still don't know who he is.'

I can guess the route Hugh has chosen, down First Avenue, left down North Street, into Washington Road and onto the seafront. We wait a while before driving down First Avenue, where we see the stranger still ahead of us, matching his pace to Hugh's. I pull up on the roadside and watch until they have both turned the corner into North Street and are out of sight.

'I've had an idea,' Libby says. 'Why don't we drive ahead of them? That way we'll get to see the man's face as he walks towards us.'

'It's a risk, they may turn down a different road, we could lose them.'

'Worth the risk?'

I nod and we pull away, driving past the stranger and Hugh. We park in front of a small row of shops.

'How about I get out of the car and wait in one of the doorways and you wait in the car?' I suggest to Libby. 'That way we have two possible angles covered.'

'What about the camera?'

'I don't think we can risk it. The flash will give us away. Let's just use our keen powers of observation,' I say and wink at her.

'I can see why you like this amateur sleuthing lark, it's fun.'

'It's not meant to be fun. We're doing a serious job here.'

As I get out of the car, the wind picks up my hair and tugs at it. I'm grateful for my hair band that keeps it from covering my eyes. Hugh turns the corner into Washington Road, but I'm certain he hasn't seen me. He has his head down, occasionally glancing behind him. I position myself well back in the doorway of *Billy's* newsagents. Hugh crosses the road and walks past the shop doorway, without a glance in my direction. Then, I hear the footsteps of the stranger approaching. Just before he is level with me I step out and walk straight into him.

'Oh, I'm so sorry, I didn't realise...' I say, staring at the face of someone I recognise. We haven't been introduced, but I know who this man is. I know because I've seen him before, at the vets. The mysterious stranger following Hugh is Mr Kenneth Elm.

When I get back in the car and report the discovery to Libby, there is disappointment on her face. Clearly, she would have liked to be the one to solve the mystery of Hugh's elusive follower. We drive back to *Jefferson's* to mull over our findings. This evening the café is heaving and the music is loud. It's like walking into a nightclub, but instead of a dance floor there are twenty or so tables, crammed with people. It's as well that Richie has help on busier nights, but the chap who approaches our table is a new face and I can tell from Libby's expression that she is instantly smitten.

'Crikey,' she says, when he moves away from us, having taken our order. 'What a dish.'

'Not bad, but not my type.'

'Good job too, consider him taken. Besides, you're well and truly spoken for. How is that husband of yours? Have you told him what you're up to?'

'Not yet, but I will. I'm waiting for the right moment.'

'Maybe there won't be one? Anyway, what happened with Kenneth, did he say anything?'

'No, he just mumbled an apology and carried on walking.'

'Will he think it's odd, you hanging around in shop doorways on a Saturday night?'

'I could have just finished stock-taking.'

'You have a vivid imagination. Must be down to all those crime novels you've spent your life reading. So, you know him?'

'No, I've seen him at the vets, when I've taken Charlie there, but I've never spoken to him.'

'Why is he following Hugh?'

'He must know that Hugh is searching for Dorothy. Maybe he's protecting her, perhaps she's hiding away in his house?'

'Why doesn't he just confront Hugh? It's weird, why would he keep following him night after night? He must have realised Hugh has seen him, it's not like he's very discreet? There's something else, Janie.'

'What?'

'Hugh has told you Dorothy is in danger, what if he's the danger?'

'Who, Kenneth?'

'No, silly, I mean what if the real reason Hugh wants you to track her down is because he wants to confront her about something, not because he's worried about her at all. Maybe that's why he's so tight-lipped and maybe that's why Kenneth is following him.'

'I'll talk to Hugh and tell him what we've discovered and see what he says.'

'Let me know.'

'Don't worry, I will.'

When Hugh strides into the library van the next day he looks hopeful.

'Did it work?' he says. 'Your plan to follow me. Did you find out who is pursuing me?'

'Take a seat for a moment.' I pull out the spare chair that I keep behind the counter, unfold it and offer it to him. He shakes his head.

'It's Kenneth, Dorothy's brother,' I say, watching his face for a reaction.

He turns away, down the length of the van, as though he is trying to gather his thoughts before replying. 'I thought as much,' he says.

'Why would he follow you? Do you have any idea? Why doesn't he just speak to you?'

He doesn't respond, but his expression shows his discomfort.

'Hugh, you say Dorothy is in danger. Surely her brother would want to protect her. Now you know who he is and where you can find him, why don't you talk to him? Tell him your concerns and let him warn her about whatever it is you are scared about? Isn't that the best way forward?'

'You don't understand, it's more complicated than that,' he says.

'I can't help you unless you are straight with me, unless you tell me the truth. Are you telling me the truth?'

He studies my face, as though he is trying to decide what to say next.

Before he speaks I say, 'The *Tidehaven Observer* has agreed to print a nostalgia feature, encouraging people to write in about their wartime experiences. We thought it might help to flush Dorothy out, or at least people who know her.'

'We?'

'I have a friend who works for the local paper, she is helping me. But I need much more from you Hugh. If you want me to succeed you're going to have to tell me what you know.'

Before he can reply, the door to the van opens and Ethel Latimer, the mother of the asthmatic child, returns.

'Bobby is no better,' she says, approaching the counter. 'It's got so that we have to sit up all night with him.' She appears to be oblivious to Hugh standing there, with his mouth open, poised to tell me what I need to know.

'I'm sorry to hear that,' I say, wondering where Bobby is while his mother is looking at books.

'I've left him with a neighbour,' she says, reading my thoughts. 'I had to pop back, even though it's further for me to come when you're parked down here on Milburn Avenue. I don't know what I was thinking the other day, when I was last in, but I didn't swap my husband's book. It's important he has a book to read.'

A host of questions appear in my head. Should her husband be expecting her to swap in his library book if it means leaving poor Bobby with a neighbour? She is speaking, but I've missed what she's said. I need to focus. Perhaps Bean is affecting my concentration, as well as my digestion. Mrs Latimer likes to chat. But chatting often leads to gossip and gossip can be dangerous when it comes to objective thinking. I guide her to the shelf laden with thrillers, hoping to return to speak to Hugh in peace, but when I turn around he has gone.

Chapter 9

Every couple of months there is a changeover of books in the mobile library. Customers put in their requests and some of the books are exchanged from the main library, while others are ordered in as new titles. On book changeover day I call into the main library at the start of my shift and, with the janitor's help, load the boxes of new books into the van. During the day I use any spare time to re-order the shelves, filtering out the less popular books to make space for the new ones.

This month's batch of books holds a couple of delights for me, with two new Agatha Christie novels, plus Alastair McLean's *Force 10 from Navarone,* which I'm certain Greg will love. I'm in the middle of sorting the crime shelves when I hear a friendly voice.

'I've got something to show you,' Phyllis says, putting her shopping bag down on the counter. 'Oh, excellent, new books. Anything that might take my fancy?'

'Take a look, but you can't have Agatha, at least until I've finished with her.'

'I wouldn't dream of depriving you. I'm guessing you'll be needing every ounce of Poirot's genius to help with your new case. I'm assuming you've decided to take it on, despite everything?'

'Everything, being Greg and Bean?' She won't have missed the edge to my voice. 'I've seen the most beautiful pram.'

'Ah, a good incentive then. Come and look at this, I've found a photo.' She pulls an envelope from her bag and hands it to me. I take out the black and white photo and hold it close to the desk-light.

'Kenneth Elm?'

'Spot on. When you mentioned the father with bronchitis, it triggered a memory. I've got photos of several of my class groups and, to be completely honest with you, the names and faces are starting to merge. It's no fun getting old, you know.'

'Rubbish, you're still a youngster.'

'Well, I retrieved my box of photos from the loft, rifled through them and there it was.'

'I need a magnifying glass.'

'I know the photo isn't great, one of the teachers took it on their box Brownie. It was the school play. We'd encouraged Kenneth to get involved. He wasn't the most confident of children. He had a minor role, but his father approached me afterwards, asking if I thought he had potential.'

'To be an actor?'

'I had to let him down gently.'

'Was he a bright student?'

'Average, as I recall. But keen and very polite.'

'He's a vet now.'

'I thought you didn't know anything about him?'

'Yes, well, I didn't, but then I took Charlie to the vet for dad and there was his name, on the board.'

'Have you met him?'

'No, that's the next challenge.' Now is not the time to mention secret moonlit pursuits.

'So, my photo doesn't help then?'

'Of course it does. Everything helps. It might give me an intro. You know that Poirot says, "*Beware! Peril to the detective who says: It is so small - it does not matter. That way lies confusion! Everything matters.*"'

'Good for Poirot. So, a vet, well, he did better than I would have imagined.'

'What about his sister? She wasn't at your school? Her name is Dorothy, she was a couple of years older.'

'Sorry, no I don't think so. Now I've remembered Kenneth, I'm certain I would recall if I'd met his sister. She must have been at the secondary modern. What's this?' she says, turning to read Libby's poster. I've pinned it on the cork board beside the counter. Phyllis reads it aloud.

Tidehaven Observer celebrates the past
Prepare for Remembrance Sunday by
sharing your wartime anecdotes with us

A selection of letters will appear in a
special double-page spread on November 6th
We'd love to hear from you.

'Libby's idea,' I say.

'To help with your case?'

'Er, kind of, yes.'

'Mm,' is all she says and I'm left wondering if her silence means disapproval, or if she is as intrigued as I am to know more about the Elm family.

On my days with dad I check through his post, which is usually an assortment of bills and the occasional thank you card from a grateful patient. Even though he can't see them, I've created a sort of montage with all the ones he's received over the years. It's good PR, I tell him, although he doesn't need any marketing or promotion. His waiting list speaks for itself.

But today we have a happy surprise among the assortment that has landed on the doormat.

'Hey, dad, how about this? We've got a card from Aunt Jessica.'

'Excellent. Where is she? What does she say?'

The postcard carries an Italian stamp and the caption on the front reads, *Saluti da Roma*. The photo is divided in four, showing the Colosseum, St Peter's Basilica, the Trevi Fountain and the Spanish Steps.

'Hooray, she's coming to see us. Listen to this,' I say, reading her note aloud:

'Dear Philip and Janie, it's high time we had a catch up and as it's not so easy for you to come to me, then it looks like I'll have to brave your English winter and head to Tamarisk Bay. I thought we could have Christmas together. What do you think? Write to me c/o Ufficio Postale, Piazzale Orazio, Anzio and let me know. Lots of love, Jessica.'

'Well, that's a turn up,' dad says.

'You don't think there's a problem, do you? Is that why she needs to come back?'

'She's not coming back, she's visiting for Christmas. She'll have a real surprise when she sees that bump of yours.'

Aunt Jessica stepped into the breach when mum left and the three of us spent nine happy years together. Then, once I was old enough to look after myself, and look out for dad, she decided to leave us to it. Since then she's travelled all over Europe, sending us regular postcards and making me envious.

'Do you think she'll stay until Bean is born?' I say.

'One step at a time, love. I know you, I bet you're already planning to ask her to be godmother. Don't have too many expectations, or you'll be disappointed.'

'Think how brilliant it'll be, dad. There's years to catch up on. She can stay with us, or maybe she'd like to stay here with you. Oh, my God, I've just realised, she hasn't even met Greg. How crazy is that? But, you're right, I can't think of more perfect godparents; you, Jessica and Phyllis.'

'Aren't you forgetting something?'

'What?'

'Well, it sounds a bit one-sided. Won't Greg want to involve his family? His parents, or his sister maybe?'

My sigh was a little too obvious.

'All I'm saying is,' dad continued, 'talk to Greg, see what he thinks. It's his baby too, remember.'

Greg almost always arrives home before me and by the time I'm back he has had his bath and is relaxing in the kitchen with a cuppa. But today I race back from dad's and run a bath, carefully timed so it's still hot when he arrives sweaty and muddy at the back door.

'You're home,' he says, dropping his lunchbox in the sink. 'That's a nice surprise, everything alright?'

'Absolutely. And sir has a hot bath ready and waiting for him.'

'Really?'

'Yes, I've been neglecting my husband and decided I'd better do something about it.'

'Feeling guilty, eh?' He puts his arms around me and pulls me in close to him for a hug, or at least as close as Bean will permit. 'Joining me in the bath?'

'You're joking. I'd only create a tsunami. But I'll scrub your back if you like.'

An hour or so later we're in the sitting room. I'm relaxing on the sofa, with my feet on his lap and my head snuggled into one of the cushions.

'Guess what?'

'What?'

'Aunt Jessica - she's coming home for Christmas. She sent a postcard. She's in Italy, lucky thing.'

'Excellent. I'll finally get to meet her.'

'And she'll get to meet you, and maybe Bean.'

'Will she stay on then? Into next year?'

'I hope so. Imagine, if she does we could ask her to be the other godmother.'

He lifts my feet off his lap, extricates himself and turns to face me.

'The other godmother?'

'Yes. Phyllis is one and then Jessica.'

'When was this decided?'

He may have been warm from the bath, but there was now a distinct chill in the air.

'It makes perfect sense,' I say, trying not to sound defensive. 'Phyllis is like my grandmother and well, Jessica virtually brought me up. You know how close I was to her.'

'And who are you planning for godfather? Your dad, I suppose?'

I bite my lip and try to calculate a response that will ease the mounting tension.

'Is this how it's going to be?' he says, glaring at me.

'What?'

'Do you intend to make all the decisions about our child? I'm only the father, after all.'

'Don't be like that. Of course I want your opinion. Let's not row. I know, why don't we have loads of godparents? Who would you like? Your mum and dad? We could ask them too. Bean will love having loads of people looking out for him - or her.'

'What about Becca? Don't you think she'll want to be involved with her big brother's first child? I'll tell them they're the reserves, shall I? The also-rans?'

'Come on, now you're being silly.'

'And you're being selfish.' He pulls away from me, stands up and walks out of the room. I hear him put his jacket on and when I go out into the hall, he's standing by the front door.

'Where are you going? We haven't had supper yet.'

'The pub. Don't bother with supper, I'll get something there.'

'Let's talk about it some more,' I say, but my voice is drowned out by the noise of the door slamming.

Chapter 10

At breakfast the next morning I'm trying to think of the best way to raise the subject of godparents again, without causing another row. Instead, Greg comes up behind me and kisses the back of my neck.

'I'm not sure I deserve that. I've been mean and thoughtless, haven't I?' I say, turning to return the kiss.

'Well, if you want to put it like that,' he says, smiling. 'Just don't shut me out, we're a partnership, remember?'

'You're right and I'm sorry, really. Am I forgiven?'

'You're in luck because my pub visit last night has put me in an excellent mood. Alex managed to get a pair of tickets for the match. I don't know how he did it, but I've told him there's a pint in it for him, at the very least.'

'This Saturday?' I ask.

'Yes, Brighton, at home. Should be brilliant.'

'If they win.'

'Of course they'll win.'

'Says their biggest fan.'

My immediate thought is a free Saturday to do more investigating, but then alarm bells start ringing in my head. Maybe it's time to share more than godparent decisions with Greg.

The letters have started to arrive for Libby's nostalgia feature and now I understand why her editor suggested she sort through them in her own time. We take it in turns to read some aloud to each other. Our emotions swing from sadness, through incredulity, to joy. The same emotions that many families must have experienced during the terror of the bombings, when they received news that a missing loved one was safe.

'Living through a world war must have changed that generation forever,' I say, taking a bite of my sandwich. Libby and I are spending lunchtimes together in the library van, with the *Closed* sign posted on the door so we are not disturbed. 'I wouldn't have coped. Young men sent off to blow other people up, with only a few months' experience of handling weapons. Mothers having to let their children be evacuated to live with strangers. And the little ones, imagine how terrified they must have been.'

'We only just missed it, if we'd been born a few years earlier that could have been us, being sent off to some strange village with our little suitcase and name badge.'

'I can understand why dad doesn't talk about it.'

'Interesting how many people do want to share their memories though. Maybe it's easier writing it down?'

The realisation that Dorothy has chosen not to write in doesn't surprise me. I would have been more surprised if she had. Libby is disappointed, even though her editor is delighted with the response and has promised her a bonus for coming up with the idea.

'No mention of a day off in lieu for all the hours I've spent trawling through misspelled tirades,' she says, sounding disgruntled. 'Some of these people write as though they're the only ones affected. They seem to forget it was a world war.'

'Remember that education back then wasn't like it is now. Children often didn't start school until they were six or seven. No wonder their spelling isn't perfect.'

'You think I'm heartless, don't you?'

'Maybe you have to be in your line of work.'

'What about yours then?'

'What, being a librarian?'

'No, I mean being a private investigator. That's what you are now you know, you're being paid, so that makes it official.'

'I try to remain objective, not jump to conclusions. Hopefully, I don't let my emotions cloud my judgement, but that's not the same as being heartless. And, no, I don't think you are, well not all the time, anyway.'

I can hear people talking outside the van and a check of my watch tells me that my lunch-break is over. 'I'm going to call round to see Hugh later. I'll tell him about the letters, that nothing significant has turned up and try to pin him down about the real reason for tracking Dorothy down. You're right that he's hiding something.'

'There's something else I'm right about. Put your hands out on the counter.'

'What?'

'Both hands, put them both flat down. There, I knew it. You've started biting your nails.'

'Er, yes, guilty as charged.'

'A new and disgusting habit, or a return to some childhood fetish?'

'Aunt Jessica cured me of it by rubbing lemon juice on them when I was little. I used to bite them right down to the quick, making them bleed sometimes.'

'And now you've started again?'

'Mm, trouble is I like lemon juice now, so that won't work, will it?'

'I've got a better idea. I'll paint them for you. You'll hardly want to munch your way through coats of nail varnish, will you? Is that a deal?'

'Deal,' I say, closing my hands into fists to hide my fingers.

'What about Hugh, he'll want to know what you're going to do next.'

'I'll tell him my plans are fluid.'

'Non-existent, in other words?' she winks, throws her bag over her shoulder and leaves.

Although Hugh mentioned his landlady, Mrs Summer, I have yet to meet her. She answers the door promptly and I'm a little taken aback to see a woman in her early forties, with jet black hair and deeply bronzed skin. She is stylishly dressed in a mustard coloured shift dress, with a white linen collar and a string of dark brown beads dangling down the front of the dress. Another reminder, should I need one, that it is never wise to make assumptions. Clearly, landladies come in all shapes and sizes.

'Hello there,' I say, 'I wonder if I could speak to Mr Furness? He said it would be alright to call in.'

She studies me carefully, but doesn't move back or invite me in. As I stand on the doorstep, I recall Hugh's suggestion that I can pretend I am his niece. But, at this stage, I'd rather not fabricate too many stories. Mrs Summer could easily turn up at the library van one day and the whole thing could escalate out of control.

'You are?' she says, still holding the door only slightly ajar.

'Janie Juke. I'm a friend of Mr Furness. Well, a friend of the family.' This white lie seems like a good compromise.

'Come in a moment, please,' she stands back, opens the door fully and beckons me in.

'Is he in?' I ask her. 'Don't worry if not, I can leave a message if that's okay with you.'

'He is in hospital.' She articulates her words, as though she is making a public announcement. I detect an accent, possibly European, or perhaps further afield.

'Oh, I'm sorry. Has he had an accident?'

'His chest,' she says, laying her hands on her own chest to emphasise the point. 'This morning he could not breathe. I called an ambulance. It was very frightening.'

'Goodness, yes, it must have been. Will he be alright? What did the ambulancemen say?'

'They took him away. They gave him oxygen. They put a mask on him and he kept pushing it away. He was very upset.'

It's hard to take in all that she is telling me, particularly as the more she speaks the more agitated she becomes and with her agitation her accent grows stronger.

'I know he has chest problems, but I hadn't realised it was so serious,' I say.

'Will you tell his family?'

'His family?'

'You said you are a friend of his family. I have no contact details. They will be worried.'

This is exactly the kind of confusion I was trying to avoid. I choose to sidestep her question. 'I'll go to the hospital, see how he is. Shall I let you know?'

'He should stay in hospital. Perhaps he should not come back.'

'Are you saying you won't keep his room?'

She shrugs her shoulders, but doesn't respond.

I catch the bus to St Richard's and enquire at the main reception desk. I am told that Mr Hugh Furness was admitted earlier in the day and is in Charlotte Ward. Fortunately, I have arrived during visiting hours, so I make my way to the ward. It's only as I approach Hugh's bed that I realise I haven't brought anything with me, no grapes, no sweets, not even a newspaper. He is sitting up, with no pipes or tubes in evidence.

'Well, that's a relief,' I say, pulling up a chair to his bedside. 'Mrs Summer had me worried. Sounds as though you had a nasty episode this morning. Feeling better now?'

'Good of you to come,' he says, speaking slowly and quietly, taking small breaths in-between each word.

'I'm sorry I haven't brought you anything, it was all a bit of a rush. I wanted to catch visiting hours. You know what these Matrons are like. Dragons, or so I've heard.'

'The nurses have been extremely kind. I gave poor Mrs Summer a shock. It's the worst episode I've had for a while.'

'How long have you had your lung condition? Is the treatment not helping?'

'There isn't much they can do. I'm supposed to stay calm, anxiety exacerbates it. But this search for Dorothy...do you have news for me?'

I pour Hugh a glass of water from the jug on his bedside table.

'I'll pop out and get myself a glass, back in a second.' I wander out to the little kitchen area outside the ward, taking my time so that I can decide on the best approach. Whatever I say, or don't say, could well trigger another attack for Hugh. My actions could affect the health of my client. I'm beginning to wish I'd never taken his case on and yet there is a vulnerability about Hugh, a sadness that I can't quite make out. Perhaps I'm a sucker for lost souls.

Returning to Hugh's bedside I pour myself some water and sit down. He is looking expectantly at me.

'Hugh, I told you about the nostalgia feature, didn't I?'

He nods. 'Has something cropped up? Have you heard from Dorothy?'

'We're still working our way through the correspondence. But you mentioned there was more you could tell me about Dorothy, about the time you had with her, during the war. Are you able to talk about it?'

'I told you. We met and once the war ended I didn't see her again.'

'There must have been more to it than that?'

'I was a pilot,' he says.

'Yes, I know. You said you were in the RAF and Dorothy was a land girl, that's right, isn't it?'

He nods and closes his eyes. He is quiet for a moment and I wonder if the memories are too difficult for him. Then he starts to speak. His words come out slowly, interspersed with small breaths. Throughout his explanation I watch him, scared that as his story unfolds the trauma of his memories will trigger another coughing attack. One of the ward nurses is hovering in the background. I'm grateful she is there, in case I need to call her.

'I was more than just a pilot,' he says.

'Were you a squadron leader?'

He hesitates as though he is struggling to find the right words. 'Have you heard of the SOE?'

'No, were they a special air forces division?'

'In a way, but not only the air force. The Special Operations Executive were recruited from across all types of people, military personnel as well as civilians. It was a secret organisation, designed to create havoc, undermine the enemy in ways they would least expect.'

'And you were part of it?'

'Let's just say I worked with them on occasion.'

'What did you have to do?'

'When the conditions were right I would be tasked to fly an operative into northern France. The French resistance were doing a marvellous job in the face of terrific danger, and the SOE gave us a chance to help them.'

'So the people you flew in, the operatives, what did they have to do?'

'We were never told. You have to understand this was a secret organisation, everything was on a need to know basis. All I ever needed to know was where and when. Flights were planned around the moon period.'

My frown encourages him to explain.

'They often chose the days just before or after the full moon. It helped us with navigation and meant we could spot anything that might hamper our landing, like a river running through the middle of a field. Members of the resistance would be there at the meeting point, and they would take the Joe away.'

'The Joe?'

'That's how we referred to the operatives, we knew them as Joe. No names, no pack drill.' He stops speaking and draws a few deeper breaths. I reassure him that he doesn't have to tell me now, the rest of the story can wait until he is stronger. Although, in reality, I wonder if he ever will be stronger. Right now, it seems doubtful.

'One night I was given my orders. A sortie was planned for 22.00 hours. I prepared the plane and waited. The Joe arrived and as they climbed up into position I caught a glimpse of a face. It was a moment that will live with me forever.'

His eyes are open now, staring straight ahead. Sweat appears on his forehead and he seems unable to continue.

'Who was it Hugh? Did you recognise the person?'

He nods and in a whisper he says, 'yes, it was the woman I loved.'

My mind is whirling with questions. This new disclosure answers so much and yet leaves even more unanswered.

Before I can ask him anything else the Ward Sister announces that visiting is over and asks us all to leave. There are only two other visitors on the ward, so the three of us file out dutifully, like children en route to the playground. As I walk out into the hospital grounds I realise that once again I have failed to ask Hugh what I had planned to ask him. Although, if he and Dorothy worked with the SOE, perhaps they were privy to some critical information that must remain secret. Maybe it is the organisation itself that is putting Dorothy in danger.

Much later, I lay in bed and revisit all Hugh has told me. I'm still working through the implications, as Greg wraps his arms around me and turns off the bedside light.

'Do you think Bean will like football?' he says, any annoyance from our row about godparents long forgotten.

'Bound to.'

'Maybe he'll play.'

'Or she?'

'Um, girls playing football? Maybe not.'

'Famous netball player then, or tennis?'

The only answer I get is a throaty snore.

Chapter 11

I arrive early at dad's on Thursday morning. The kettle is already on the gas and Charlie is looking a little damp from his early morning walk.

'The birds have been at the cream again,' I say, transferring the milk from one of the bottles into a milk jug. 'How about I put out a box for the milkman, something with a lid that the little monkeys can't peck through?'

'Good idea. Maybe check with the milkman first though, when you next see him. Just in case he thinks it will make too much work for him.'

'We're having a "*godparent discussion*" this evening, apparently,' I say, passing dad his hot drink. 'Greg mentioned it as he rushed out of the door this morning.'

'Well, go easy with him, remember Bean is part of both of you.'

'Am I being selfish?'

'No, not selfish, maybe a little thoughtless sometimes.'

'Mm, that's hard to hear from my dad.'

'You couldn't be more thoughtful when it comes to looking out for me, but with Greg, well you can be a bit hard on him.'

'We're stuck in a pattern. I say something, he gets upset, we have a bit of a row, then he storms off to the pub. He sulks for a day or so, then we make up and everything's fine.'

'Relationships are organic.'

'How do you mean?'

'Well, ever changing. Shifting, like the tide going in and out. Sometimes the sea is calm, other times it's tempestuous. As long as you're both good swimmers, you'll be okay.'

'You and mum didn't like the sea much, did you? The sea of married life, I mean.'

'I guess I was happy to float in dangerous waters and she didn't see herself as a lifeguard.'

'Mm,' I say, mulling over what dad has said, as well as what he hasn't.

'So, the godparent discussion,' dad says. 'Do you know how you'll approach it? What do you think Greg is hoping for?'

'I'll let him do the talking, I'll listen carefully and aim for a fifty-fifty result, fair to all parties.'

Dad smiles, as I add, 'Thank goodness we only have to go through this once.'

'You don't know that, who knows what the future holds,' he says.

'Oh yes, that is one thing I do know for certain. Anyway, on another subject, I need to do some research and you're just the man for it.'

'First patient due in forty-five minutes. Enough time to complete your research?'

'Possibly. Stage one, at least. What do you know about the Special Operations Executive? Have you heard of it?'

'Goodness. Well, as I understand it they were our secret weapon during the war. Churchill's Secret Army it was known as, I think. They got involved in all sorts of clandestine operations, blowing up bridges, sabotaging supply chains. They even created dummy airfields to confuse German reconnaissance. Why?'

'It turns out Hugh wasn't just another pilot. He worked with the SOE.'

'I'm amazed he told you.'

'Me too. He's so desperate to find Dorothy that he wants to prove he trusts me, I suppose.'

'Why is it relevant?'

'Well, he flew occasional sorties for the SOE, flying SOE operatives into France and recovering them too sometimes.'

'It must have been extremely dangerous.'

'Incredibly. I've scoured our reference section in the library, but I could only find one book, it was an account of the work they did in France.'

'Handy to be working in a library?'

'My workplace has taken on a whole new meaning. Imagine what Poirot could have done with access to all that background information. Although most of the time he didn't seem to need it.'

'His knowledge came from experience, you're a touch younger than him, remember?'

'Well, the book backed up what Hugh told me, the operations were meticulously planned, they'd choose a day just before or after a full moon.'

'The clear conditions would have helped with their visibility, and yet at the same time made them more visible.'

'Yes, imagine the risks they had to take and the French resistance too. These were people just like you and me and yet they were prepared to endanger their lives on a daily basis.'

While we have been talking Charlie has stretched himself out between the two of us, rolled onto one side and drifted off into a deep sleep. Now we are distracted for a moment as he twitches and growls, no doubt chasing an imaginary rabbit across a field and into its burrow.

'I told you about Dorothy,' I continue, 'the woman he wants me to track down? Well, Hugh and Dorothy had been seeing each other, dancing and...'

'They were in love?'

'That's what he said, yes.'

'Anyway, one night Hugh is due to fly an operative into France. Everything was anonymous; they were all known as 'Joe'. So, Hugh prepares himself and his plane, and the Joe arrives, dressed in overalls, camouflage, I suppose. It was dark, of course, so he assumes it's a man. It was only when he saw the face up close, he discovered it was Dorothy.'

'But I thought she was a land girl?'

'She was. All SOE operatives worked undercover, they had ordinary jobs, lived ordinary lives, until the moment they had to go into action. Because of all the secrecy, neither of them knew the truth. It must have been such a shock.'

'For both of them. And for Hugh, imagine having to leave the girl you love in the middle of occupied France, never knowing if she was going to be taken prisoner, or worse. What happened?'

'Well, that's the saddest part. She had her orders, but everything had to be secret. Even though Hugh worked with the SOE as well, she couldn't tell him anything.'

'Need to know, and all that.'

'Exactly. All he knew was the location where he had been told to leave her. He flew her out there, landed in the field and members of the resistance met her and that was it. He didn't see her again.'

Before I could finish the story, my hiccups decide to intervene. Imagining Hugh and Dorothy's plight was clearly too much for my anxiety levels.

'Drink some water, take a breath,' dad says. 'Do you think Hugh is being straight with you? He is clearly an expert at keeping secrets, maybe there's more to this story that he isn't sharing with you. He's told you Dorothy is in danger, do you think it's to do with the SOE? By the very nature of it an organisation like that will have had its enemies.'

As I sip the water the hiccups begin to subside, allowing me to reply. 'From what I've read she was one of the lucky ones, many of the operatives were captured and sent to concentration camps. It's truly horrible, dad, they were tortured, some were executed and the terrifying thing is that many were just my age. I can't bear the thought of what they had to go through.'

'What are you mixed up with, princess? This doesn't sound at all straightforward. Maybe it's time to call a halt.'

On my next library day, I have time to think over what I've discovered so far, which isn't much. Certainly not enough to justify Hugh's down payment. In truth, all I can tick off my list is having established the identity of Hugh's mystery follower.

Call it serendipity or coincidence, but the next person to walk into the van is Kenneth Elm. I keep my head down, focusing on the pile of books on the counter, foolishly hoping he won't notice me.

'Mrs Juke?' He has a slight lisp, it's barely noticeable. Perhaps he has spent a lifetime trying to disguise it.

'Good morning, how can I help you?' I say. He knows my name; this does not bode well. He glances around the van; there are two other customers, one browsing the historical novels section and the other looking at children's books. Both are focused on their task.

'You followed me, the other evening. I'd like to know why,' he says.

My first thought is to deny it, but I don't want to insult the man's powers of observation. He saw me, he knows my name.

'I was helping a friend of mine.'

'Is he a friend? Does your father know you're chasing strange men around at night?'

'You know my father?'

'Of course, his guide dog Charlie is one of my patients. Your father is a brave and talented man. Does he know what you're up to?'

'Up to? I'm not up to anything.'

I don't attempt to hide the indignation in my voice. My hiccups are threatening again. Between my hiccups and his lisp, we make an interesting pair for any eavesdroppers.

'Why is he looking for my sister?' he says.

'What makes you think he is?'

'He's been asking around. Tamarisk Bay is a small town. When a stranger turns up and starts asking questions, word gets around.'

'He knew your sister during the war. They were friends.'

'That's not the way she remembers it.'

'You're in touch with her then? She's moved back here?'

We have to stop speaking while a customer brings his selection of books over to me for stamping. I have a brief conversation with him and Kenneth moves away, towards the first row of bookshelves. I watch him as he runs his fingers over a few of the spines, settling on one and sliding it out, only to slide it back in without opening it. Having dealt with the customer, I signal to Kenneth and he returns to the counter.

'The truth of it is he's worried about your sister.' I say, keeping my voice as low as possible, without whispering. 'He believes she's in danger.'

'The only person she's in danger from is Hugh Furness.'

'No, that's not true. He's come here especially because he's concerned for her safety.'

'Think about it. Why is he being so clandestine? Why involve you at all? If he was really concerned about her, why not approach me directly, or better still speak to the police?'

There are still times when I wish I was a little girl again, with my hero dad beside me. This is definitely one of them. I have no idea which of these men is telling the truth. If Kenneth is right, I've got myself mixed up with a liar, at the very least, maybe far worse. On the other hand, if I'm to believe Hugh, a woman's life could be in danger. I can't sit and do nothing.

'Why have you been following Hugh?' I ask.

'To warn him off.'

'Why didn't you just speak to him, you know where his lodgings are. Why not knock on the door and have it out with him?'

'He's a clever man. I couldn't risk him questioning me. I might have let something slip. Dorothy is my sister, she's vulnerable, it's my job to protect her. You can give your friend a message from me, and from my sister.'

'What kind of message?'

'Tell him to go back where he came from. There's nothing for him here.'

There are no options open to me. I can't talk this through with dad, because he will want to warn me off, Greg is out of the question, and Libby is so focused on getting the next scoop I can't trust her to keep quiet. For now, all I can do is watch and wait for someone to make the next move.

The nostalgia feature has been published and it has become the talking point of all my library customers. So much so, I've pinned one of the spreads on the cork noticeboard that hangs beside the counter. Some of the customers are keen to tell me their stories, some have written in to the paper, but others are happy to talk.

As I listen to their tales I try to imagine what it was like living in fear every day for years. I jot down a few of their anecdotes in my notebook, immersing myself in that time, with its mixture of desperation and joy.

'The air raid siren was rising and falling for the alarm, and plain straight for the All Clear. This sort of sound still turns my stomach more than twenty years later.'

'Mother made us siren suits, one-piece with leggings, tops and hoods, out of old blankets to slip over our nightdresses when we had to run through the neighbouring gardens to the shelter. They weren't warm enough. I made up a little suitcase to take with me to the shelter, in case our house was destroyed. It contained a Bible, because that seemed to me to be appropriate to the occasion, a handkerchief, because I had a horror of being without one (!!) What else? Perhaps a drink of some sort. I forget.'

'We were always hungry. Grandad gave us fish off his boat. He showed me how to catch eels and flounders on the foreshore. Uncle Joey caught rabbits, I helped kill and skin them. With the other Grandad I collected eggs from his chickens. Auntie Lilly had a world map on the wall. She stuck flags in it and would tell us how the war was going in Russia and the Far East especially.'

'When our house was bombed we were lucky to live, the neighbours, and the rest of the family looked after us really well. The bomb didn't hit the house but fell into the garden. It was a good job we didn't make it out into the shelter because we would have been dead for sure. Both of the Grandmas turned up. One had walked about six or seven miles because no buses were running. They saw the house first and

thought we were goners so there was a lot of crying and hugging. Then we went to stay with one of the Grandmas.'

Later in the day, just as my conversational energy is flagging, Phyllis walks in.

'You look tired,' she says. 'Bean keeping you awake?'

'Amongst other things.'

'Any luck with you know who?'

I smile at Phyllis's attempt at secrecy. From the twinkle in her eye I get the feeling she is enjoying being on the edges of a mystery. Before I can reply she turns to the noticeboard.

'Interesting article, it brought back many memories. Some good, some not so good,' she says.

'What was it like for you? Did you carry on teaching throughout the war?'

'We had trainloads of evacuees. Poor little mites. Spilling out of the carriages, onto the platform, looking as frightened as baby rabbits. Some of them were barely bigger than their suitcases.'

'Did you take any to live with you?'

'Yes, a brother and sister. Both younger than Cynthia. Put her nose right out of joint, but I told her how lucky she was not to be one of them.'

'How long were they with you?'

'They came from London. They'd never seen the sea. The first weekend I took them to the beach they ran straight into the water, clothes and all. Didn't even take their shoes off.'

Phyllis takes a handkerchief from her handbag and wipes her reading glasses, before putting them away. 'By the end of their stay Cynthia loved having them around.

She wept when they left. Promised she'd write to them every day.'

'Did she stay in touch?'

'For a while, but life takes over, doesn't it?'

'Do you know where they are now? If they're still in London?'

She shakes her head.

'It must have been hard to concentrate on education with bombs falling all around.'

'Some days we didn't even try. There was such an influx of evacuees we had to use any available space for lessons. We even used the tearooms in Tensing Gardens a few times.'

'That old shack?'

'The children loved it, especially the ones from the inner cities. All that grass to run about on and all those trees to climb.' She has been leaning up against the counter, but now she moves to one side and says, 'Do you mind if I sit down for a while?'

'Here you go,' I say, passing her the spare chair. 'Let's both take the weight off. My legs get tired carrying Bean around all day.'

'Wait until he's born.'

'He?'

'Well, he or she. Do you have a preference?'

'No, ten fingers, ten toes and not too much screaming. That's all I have on my wish list.'

'You'll make a great mum.'

'Will I? There are times when I'm not so sure.'

'Well, you can't send it back, too late for that.'

'Phyllis, I'm in a quandary.'

'With your case?'

'Yes. I'm not sure who to believe.'

'What do your instincts tell you?'

I lay my hands on my midriff, enjoying the sensation of Bean's gentle movements.

'Your instincts are good,' she says, 'trust them.'

Chapter 12

Before going home, I call round to Hugh's lodgings. Mrs Summer invites me straight in.

'I am pleased you called,' she says. 'I am worried. I ring the hospital this morning and they say he is no better, no worse. They say, I am not family, they can't tell me.' She gestures to me to follow her through to the sitting room. 'Sit down please, would you like a drink?'

I'm still trying to work out her accent. 'No, I'm fine thanks. I was hoping there would be some improvement,' I say. 'I wonder how long they'll keep him in?'

'What about his family? Have you spoken to them?'

I shake my head. I'm not lying if I say no. After all, I don't even know if Hugh has any family still alive.

'I'll visit him again and let you know if there's any significant change.'

'Please tell him that, of course, I will keep his room for him.'

'Oh, I thought you said...'

'I was very harsh before. It was a shock, seeing him like that, the coughing, the breathing. It all came back.'

I raise an eyebrow and wait for her to explain.

'My husband. We weren't married long. They said it was the cigarettes, but I'm sure it was his job.'

'What did your husband do?'

'Labourer at the gas works. The money was good, but it was dangerous work. It got into his lungs. We had bought this house a little before he... I had to find a way to pay the bills. I don't like having lodgers, but...'

'We all do what we can to make ends meet.'

'You run the library?'

'The mobile library, yes.' I wonder what she might say if she knew what else I'm choosing to do to bring money in. 'Well, I'll be off then, but I'll keep in touch.'

The next opportunity I have to visit the hospital is Tuesday afternoon. The rain is thundering down and as I wait at the bus stop each car that passes seems determined to splash me. By the time the bus arrives I'm like Gene Kelly in *Singing in the Rain*. It's a short walk at the other end. I don't even bother opening my umbrella, as the wind would more than likely turn me into Mary Poppins. Two reminders in quick succession that it's time Greg and I went to the cinema.

By the time I walk into the hospital entrance, I'm dripping wet, so I stand for a while in the doorway to let the worst of the water drop off me. I can imagine Matron's disdain if I drip rain water all over her pristine lino.

Feeling a touch more presentable, I start to make my way to the ward and notice someone ahead of me in the corridor. He is walking with a purposeful stride, but he doesn't need to turn around for me to know who he is. I speed up so that I'm alongside him.

'Mr Elm,' I say, studying his expression to determine if it is one of surprise or annoyance.

'Mrs Juke.'

'Visiting someone?'

'Why else would I be here?'

'Perhaps for an appointment?'

'And you?' he says. 'All well with the baby, I hope?' He has a way of speaking that is clipped, emotionless. Maybe a technique to disguise his lisp.

'I think we both know why I'm here. And I'd hazard a guess you're here for the same reason. Hugh is very poorly you know. Any over excitement could bring on another attack.'

We have reached the entrance to the ward and we hesitate at the door.

'Only one visitor at a time at the bedside, I think,' I say, pivoting around and walking over to the two chairs that are positioned near to the ward entrance. 'Why don't you go in first, I'm happy to wait. But go easy on him, don't do anything you'll regret.'

'I think you are out of your league here, Mrs Juke. Go home, concentrate on your husband, your baby.'

Kenneth Elm can join the list of men who think they can tell me what to do; Greg, Frank Bright, even dad. Kenneth's patronising attitude makes me more determined to see the case through, even if my paying client is lying.

Ten minutes later, the ward door swings open and Kenneth strides out.

'He's all yours,' he says, with vehemence, the lisp no longer disguised.

There's no time for me to reply, as he sweeps past me and thumps down the corridor out of sight.

Hospitals are warm, often stuffy, places, with an all-pervasive odour of disinfectant. Not an environment conducive to a pregnant woman, with a queasy constitution. However, the perspiration now coating my body is likely to have nothing to do with the temperature. I push the ward door open tentatively and approach Hugh's bed. The curtains are drawn around him and I can hear voices, which though muffled, sound anxious.

'Who allowed him in here?' says a female voice, with clipped tones.

'I'm sorry, Sister, I didn't realise...' A younger voice, this time.

'This is not the time or place for your apologies, come to my office when you finish your shift. For now, please stay with Mr Furness and no visitors. You understand?'

With that, the Ward Sister pulls the curtain aside and steps out. As she moves away from the bed, I catch a glimpse of Hugh, lying down, with eyes closed and an oxygen mask over his face.

'What are you doing here?' she says, glaring at me. I have visions of being asked to stay behind after class to write *I will not eavesdrop* fifty times.

'Er, I was here to visit Mr Furness,' I say, in my most soothing voice.

'No visitors,' she says, articulating clearly as though I was a foreigner, or hard of hearing.

'Can I come back later? To see how he is?'

'No visitors until further notice. Now, out, out.' She ushers me out of the ward as though I'm a naughty child, loitering somewhere I'm not supposed to be.

Before catching the bus home, I need to calm myself and make some notes. There's a café near to the bus stop. I push the door open, hoping they are not about to close up.

'Are you still serving?' I say.

'Come in love, take the weight off.'

My relief is palpable. A friendly voice, a smile and the smell of home baking.

'This is what we need, Bean,' I whisper and put my hand on my midriff.

'What'll it be?' the waitress asks, moving a strand of her hair back from her flushed face. 'Sit yourself down, I'll bring it over. You look like you could do with a bite to eat. How about a delicious piece of bread pudding? Just made it this morning.'

'Perfect, thank you. And coffee, please.'

There are no other customers, but I choose a corner table, as far away from the counter as possible, in case my arrival sparks a flurry of trade. The waitress brings over the coffee and a more than generous slice of warmed bread pudding. A waft of nutmeg and cinnamon makes my mouth water. I can see my appetite for supper diminishing rapidly; something else I'll need to explain to Greg.

I take my notebook out and leaf through the pages. Some of the sections are almost full, while others remain blank. I am certain Hugh is still hiding something from me. What's more, he has yet to explain the relevance of the left luggage ticket, which is nestling inside my lost property box in the library van. There are three distinct questions I need answers for: why does Hugh believe Dorothy is in danger; why does Kenneth believe Hugh is lying; and why doesn't Hugh want to involve the police?

Now that Hugh is too poorly to talk, I need to find another way of filling in the blanks. Kenneth is my only link with Dorothy and he has made it clear he is not keen to speak to me. Right now, I would say the feeling is mutual.

Over the next couple of days, I mull over events so far. I may not be a brilliant judge of character (my experiences with Zara proved that) but surely a man who cares for animals can't be all bad? There has to be a reason that Kenneth is trying to protect Dorothy by keeping Hugh away. I just need to find out what it is.

Everything I've learned from Poirot has taught me that it's useful to dig around in someone's past. If I can piece together a clearer picture of the Elm family, I may unearth some clues.

At the next opportunity I call round to see Phyllis.

'How did you know I was hoping you'd call,' she says, as she welcomes me in.

'Baking day?' I ask, noticing the apron.

'Cleaning day, extremely boring, but it has to be done. However, I do have chocolate digestives.'

'I've come to tap your brains, well, actually to dig around in your memory.'

'Tap and dig away.'

'The Elms. What else do you remember about them?'

As we settle in Phyllis's lounge, in front of her coal fire, with coffee and biscuits, I am reminded that this is the experience I want for Bean. I may not be a traditional mother, at least as far as Greg and my mother-in-law are concerned, but my relationship with Phyllis proves to me that family doesn't only mean blood relatives. Shared memories, shared dreams, can bind us together just as tightly, maybe even more so.

'Since I tracked down that photo of Kenneth and his classmates, the memories have been flooding back,' Phyllis says. 'I even had a dream about him the other day. Most bizarre.'

'Was it a bad dream?'

'Oh, it was something and nothing. Probably more to do with my having a chunk of cheese after supper. Anyway, I've remembered more about Kenneth's parents. I'm not sure if it will help you much.'

'All information is useful. Did Poirot say that? If not, he should have.'

'You'll be writing your own crime novels next. A thinly disguised memoir - *The Janie Juke Crime Mysteries*.'

'Fifty years from now, maybe. You need to be old to write a memoir, don't you?'

'You're not suggesting I attempt one, are you?'

'I keep telling you, you will never be old, not in my eyes.'

She smiles and shakes her head. 'Well, Kenneth's parents. As you know, his father had chronic bronchitis. He'd worked in a factory near Peterborough. He was semi-skilled, I think. Whatever his trade was, he wasn't able to transfer easily when they moved. The doctor had advised him to move south, to live near the sea, if he wanted to live past sixty.'

'What age was he when he came to Tamarisk Bay?'

'He would have been late forties or early fifties maybe. Perhaps he fought in the Great War, but he would have been too old for the Second World War, even if his health had improved. As I recall, when they first moved down he worked for a removal firm, Pickford's probably. But he had so many days off sick they sacked him. It wasn't like it is now, people didn't have any employment protection and there was no National Health Service. So, if you couldn't afford the doctor, or the medicine, you had to suffer.'

'We take it for granted, free healthcare. I hate to think what it must have been like.'

'Life was desperate for families without money and there were plenty of them. Kenneth's mother had no choice but to find work, wherever she could. She got a cleaning job and took in laundry. Folk who had money were more than happy to pay others to do their chores.'

'I don't blame them, I wouldn't mind a cleaner. And someone to do the ironing.'

'Wouldn't we all?' Phyllis says and smiles. 'The work would have been physically hard, long hours, seven days a week. I remember Mrs Elm was never able to get along to parents' evenings, or school plays. That photo I showed you of Kenneth in the play. Well, she never saw him perform.'

'It must have been difficult for the children.'

'Kenneth was ashamed of his parents.'

'But his mother was doing all she could to keep the family fed and cared for.'

'Children can be very cruel. He had a bad lisp and they teased him for it. Then one day his father turned up at school, ranting and raving. He spoke to the headmaster, told him that if the bullying continued, he'd remove Kenneth from school.'

'He'd been drinking?'

She nods. 'It transpired that Kenneth's father had taken solace in alcohol. It would have been hard for him, knowing he couldn't support his own family, that his wife was the only breadwinner.'

'He would have been indignant, being a kept man. It's not much better now. Mr Elm wasn't helping though, spending his wife's earnings on beer. Did he take Kenneth out of school?'

'No, it was all bluster. But I'm fairly certain that soon after Kenneth left school, his mother died. His father didn't last long either. So, it would have been just the two of them, Kenneth and his sister.'

'I wonder how they managed for money. And then Kenneth studied to be a vet. That can't have been easy, financially.'

Phyllis nods. 'More questions than answers, but that shouldn't deter a clever investigator.'

'Mm,' I say, filing away this next batch of information in my mind. If this case is a jigsaw, I am just managing to connect the outside edges, with an awful lot of blanks remaining.

Chapter 13

The next time I visit the hospital, I approach with trepidation, expecting Matron to swoop down on me and forbid me entrance. Instead, I arrive at the ward to find the curtains around Hugh's bed pulled back, with no nursing staff immediately in evidence. Hugh is partly upright, supported from behind with several pillows. He has the oxygen mask over his nose and mouth and his eyes are closed.

Assuming he's sleeping, I pull up a chair as quietly as I can and sit beside the bed, waiting for him to wake up. Watching him lying there, his face pale, the collar of his striped pyjamas appearing above the sheet, I struggle to imagine him as he was when he met Dorothy. The years have been hard on Hugh, his face is lined and there are dark shadows under his eyes; he looks much older than dad, when there can only be a few years between them. Suddenly, I can feel my nose twitching and before I can grab my handkerchief I emit a loud sneeze. As a result, Hugh opens his eyes.

'I'm so sorry, you were sleeping. I was trying not to disturb you, but I must be allergic to hospitals,' I say and smile. 'Are you feeling a bit better?'

He nods and goes to remove the oxygen mask.

'No, don't,' I say, anticipating the Ward Sister's wrath if my presence should exacerbate his condition. 'I'll sit and keep you company for a while.'

He closes his eyes again and I take the opportunity to do the same. The ward is even stuffier than usual and I can feel myself drifting off. Suddenly, I'm being shaken awake by a hand on my shoulder. It's the young nurse who was given a verbal battering by the Ward Sister during my last visit.

'Are you okay?' she says. 'Would you like some water?'

'I can't believe I was dozing off. I've never been able to sleep sitting up, give me my bed and blankets every time.'

'Pregnancy can make you more tired than usual. How far along are you?'

'Six months, come Christmas I expect a good night's sleep will be a distant memory.'

She smiles and moves over to Hugh's bed, straightening the covers and refilling the glass of water that is on his bedside locker.

'How is he doing? He seems a little brighter than the last time I was in,' I say. 'A bit more colour in his face, but I see he's still on the oxygen.'

'Yes, it's helping a little. Are you family?'

'A friend of the family. Do you think he'll be in for much longer?'

'Oh, I'm only the nurse. It'll be up to the doctor.'

We hear the ward door open and she turns towards it. 'I must move on now. If you could try not to tire him.'

'Of course, but before you go, can I ask you about the man who was in last time, when Mr Furness took a turn for the worse?'

She looks timidly around the ward, perhaps aware that the Ward Sister could appear at any moment. 'I can't really say, patient confidentiality, you see.'

'I don't want you to tell me anything about your patient, just his visitor. Did you overhear their conversation? Were they having a row?'

She turns her back to Hugh and faces me, then she bends down and drops her voice to a whisper.

'He kept saying "*They'll never believe you*", over and over. Shouting at poor Mr Furness.'

'Was that it? Was that all he said?'

' "*You'll be the one to suffer in the end.*" That's what he said, just before he stormed off. It was terrible, he caused such a scene, upset the other patients and poor Mr Furness, well, we thought we were going to lose him.'

She looks so distressed I feel like suggesting she takes a seat while she recovers.

'It was all my fault,' she continues. Her face is flushed and her bottom lip is trembling.

I put my hand on her arm. 'Don't blame yourself. How could you have known what he was going to say or do. And there's no real harm done. Mr Furness looks as though he's perking up a bit.'

She turns around just as Hugh opens his eyes.

'Hello there, good sleep?' I say. 'I nearly dozed off myself and this kind nurse almost offered me a bed.' I smile at the nurse before she moves away to see to other patients.

Hugh beckons to me, so I stand and move closer to him.

'What is it? Did you want a drink? You're not in pain, are you?'

He shakes his head and points at the drawer in his bedside locker.

'Something in the drawer I can get for you?'

He nods and I pull open the drawer to find a small Bible (hospital property, I guess) and a pocketbook.

'Is it the book you want, Hugh?'

I remove the book and hand it to him. He opens the front cover, takes out a slip of paper and passes it to me. It's a handwritten note.

Take the left luggage ticket to Tidehaven Railway Station left luggage office. What you find there will help you understand.

'Understand what, Hugh? Will it explain why you are searching for Dorothy?'

He nods and then gives the book back to me. I return it to the drawer and when I glance up at him again he has closed his eyes and seems to have drifted off. The bell goes to signify the end of visiting hours and I leave the ward, clutching Hugh's handwritten note in my hand.

I put the left luggage ticket in my purse for safekeeping and on my next day with dad, I leave at lunchtime and catch the bus to Tidehaven. The bus is full and I manage to get the last seat downstairs, which is an enormous relief on two fronts. Sitting upstairs is like sitting in an ashtray, with all the smokers puffing away, plus I'm convinced that if the bus set off while I am climbing the stairs it would result in disaster. There are times when I look down at my bump and struggle to believe there is only one Bean in there. What's even more of a worry is that there are still nearly three months to go, by which time I am certain I will be the size an elephant. Not a pretty thought.

I had to wait a while at the bus stop and despite borrowing dad's extra-large umbrella the moisture has seeped under my collar and down my neck. Now we are well into November each day is either cold, wet, grey or windy, or a mixture of all four. Today the rain is more of a mizzle than a downpour, the kind of rain you can't see, but which soaks you nevertheless.

It's a short walk from the town centre to the railway station, which sits at the top of King's Road. It's a busy station, with a direct line to London and Brighton, but at this time of day there aren't many people about. I watch an elderly couple at the ticket office, him in a smart suit and thick overcoat, her in a camel-coloured winter coat, with a felt hat that I'm sure will spoil in the rain. They buy their tickets and then walk arm-in-arm towards the ticket barrier, off on a shopping trip, perhaps, or for afternoon tea. There is a gentle normality about them, which is at odds with the way I feel as I walk to the left luggage depository. As I approach a uniformed man glances up from his copy of the *Daily Mirror* .

'Can I help you, miss?' he says.

'I'd like to retrieve this please.'

I hand over the ticket, hoping he won't ask me what I expect to be given in return. He stares at the ticket and frowns.

'That goes back a while. Been away, have you miss?'

'Er, yes.' I prepare a tale of an imaginary trip overseas, but I hesitate to offer any further information and wait for him to make the next move.

'Won't be a moment, miss.' He walks off into the back of the depository. To one side of the counter is a row of metal lockers, large enough to store a briefcase or handbag, each distinctly numbered. Further back are long wooden racks, partly filled with suitcases and holdalls of various sizes and shapes. Finally, at the back of the depository is a long rail, where coats and jackets are hanging.

I'm trying to imagine why someone would leave a coat in left luggage, when the railwayman reappears with a large envelope in his hand.

'Just this, miss?' he says, holding it in front of me, but looking as if he is loath to release it into my hands.

'Yes, that's the one,' I say, moving forward to take it from him.

'That's two shillings and sixpence, miss,' he says, still clinging to the envelope.

'Ah, yes, of course.' I'm relieved I've got enough in my purse to pay the bill and make a mental note to add the cost to my out-of-pocket expenses.

I hand over the money and he gives me the envelope. I start to walk away, when he says, 'Just a minute, miss.' I feel like a criminal about to be found out. Instead, he says, 'Your receipt, miss. I'll write one out for you, won't take a minute.'

I nod and smile, conscious that my heart is thumping a little too energetically.

There's a small café to the side of the station. I ask for a glass of lemonade and sit at one of the metal tables on a particularly uncomfortable metal chair. The table is sticky with the residue of spilt drinks and I'm tempted to ask for a cloth to wipe it, but decide against it.

The envelope is not sealed, the flap is just tucked inside the opening. I ease it apart and slide my fingers in, pulling out a single piece of paper. It is a press cutting, a half page, carefully cut and folded in two. I lay the envelope onto the sticky tabletop and put the press cutting on top of it, in an attempt to keep it clean. One side of the paper is a collection of adverts; I recognise the names of some of the shops. I notice the date at the top of the cutting and see that it is from the *Tidehaven Observer, 19th September 1946*. On the reverse of the paper is a large photo of a group of men and women, posing in front of the Elmrock Theatre.

The headline reads: **Chess crown captured.**

The caption below the photo reads: **A local delegation supports British success.**

Staring at the photo for several minutes, I reflect on Poirot's words from *The Mysterious Affair at Styles*.

'There is something missing - a link in the chain that is not there.'

Is this photo a clue? If so, what does it mean? Why would Hugh consider it so vital that he has locked it away in left luggage? Nothing makes any sense.

Chapter 14

The *Tidehaven Observer* offices are at the opposite end of King's Road, close to the town centre. To one side of the entrance is a printed list, indicating that the newspaper is run from the third floor of the office block. I use the short journey in the lift to adjust my hair band, teasing a few knots from my hair with my fingers.

I haven't been into the *Observer* offices before, in fact, it's my first time in any newspaper office. I don't know what I'd imagined, but the first thing to take me by surprise is the quiet. Rather than a frenetic buzz of chatter and telephones ringing, there is one reporter tapping intermittently on a typewriter. Beside him are two desks, both unattended and covered with papers, scattered untidily. One of the desks has a wire filing basket, piled high with magazines and papers, which looks ready to topple over onto the floor. The strong smell of cigarette smoke rings alarm bells. I've never liked the smell, but since I've been pregnant any whiff of tobacco turns my stomach.

My arrival appears to have gone unnoticed. I take a quick glance around the room; there is no sign of Libby. Behind the untidy desks is a frosted glass partition. I can see the shadowy outline of two people, both seated and engaged in a quiet conversation. Then a phone rings and I hear Libby's voice say, '*No problem, I'll catch you later then,*' and she emerges from behind the partition.

'Janie, how lovely to see you. What brings you here? Is everything okay?'

My face must have a residual frown. The day has not turned out quite the way I had expected. Although I'm not sure what I did expect. She beckons me over to one of the desks, the one with the toppling mountain of papers.

'Come and sit down. What's happening?' she says.

Everything about Libby exudes enthusiasm. Her short, bobbed blonde hair accentuates her big blue-green eyes, expertly enhanced with eyeliner and mascara. She has a permanent beaming smile and a wide-eyed expression that reminds me of a startled fawn. Now I know what she earns, I'm intrigued as to how she manages to keep up with the latest fashion. Today she is wearing a Biba-style purple gingham mini dress, which accentuates her pencil-like figure. I'm guessing the rain we had this morning encouraged her to ditch the strappy shoes she usually wears for the white, knee-length boots that now complete her outfit.

'Not an advocate of the clean desk policy?' I say, winking.

'Not like you, eh? With your notebook and your lists. You should give me lessons.' She brushes some of the papers to one side and laughs. 'How come you're in Tidehaven? Isn't this one of your dad days?'

'I've got something to show you.' I scrabble around inside my duffel bag, take the envelope and hand it to her.

'Crikey, is it evidence?' she whispers, glancing over at her colleague who has stopped typing and is making it obvious our conversation is more interesting.

'Come on, let's take a walk,' Libby says. She stands and grabs her coat from the back of her chair.

It's a relief to be out in the fresh air. I take a few deep breaths to clear my nose and throat of the stale smoke.

'How do you stand it?' I ask her.

'What?'

'The smoke. At least you should open a few windows.'

'It's winter, or hadn't you noticed? It doesn't bother me, I'm used to it. Let's dive in here,' she says, pushing open the door to the Wimpy Bar. She looks at the row of raised stools in front of the window.

'Don't even think about it,' I say. 'When you've a bump this size, anything other than the norm is out of reach.' I head over to an empty table beside the counter. 'Your local?'

'You've discovered my secret,' she says and winks. 'Milkshake?'

I smile in agreement and she orders, then brings the drinks over to join me at the table.

'Now, what's this all about. I'm intrigued,' she says.

I push the envelope towards her and gesture to her to open it.

'Take a look and see what you think,' I say.

She opens the flap and gingerly slides out the press cutting. Spreading it flat on the table between us, she does as I did and turns it over, looking at both sides.

'An article about a chess tournament, in Tidehaven.' She peers more closely at the date. 'In 1946. Right, so how is this relevant?'

'I have no idea, but it's important enough for Hugh to secrete it in left luggage.'

'That's weird. Hasn't he told you anything else?'

'Hugh worked with a secret organisation during the war. Have you heard of the Special Operations Executive?'

'I've read bits and pieces about it, yes. Crikey, no wonder he comes across as a man of mystery. Was Dorothy caught up with the same thing. Is that why she's in danger?'

'It's possible, but now we have this cutting, I was wondering if you could do some digging around.'

'You mean professional research?'

'Er, yes. Maybe check back through the archives? Perhaps something else happened on the day of this chess tournament, maybe the date is the clue?'

'Can't you just ask Hugh?'

'He's too poorly. He could barely speak last time I saw him. He looks so vulnerable tucked up in his hospital bed. I can't help but feel sorry for him.'

'Well, in my opinion this case is a no-hoper. Your client isn't telling you what you need to know and now he's too poorly to tell you anything at all. Why not forget about it and wait for a better one to come along?'

'Oh, Libby, there's such a sadness about him and I'm certain it's not just his illness.'

'He must still be grieving for his wife?'

'Yes, there's that too. I don't know, maybe I'm developing a motherly instinct in advance of Bean's arrival.'

'He's old enough to be your dad.'

'Well, maybe I have a weakness for hopeless causes. But if you're hoping I'll take on another case after this, you can forget it. I'm going to have a baby, remember?'

'Okay, I'll have a ferret around and see what I can dig up.'

'Come and see me in the library tomorrow? Let me know what you've found?'

'Crikey, you believe in cracking the whip. I'm not sure I can drop everything, just like that.'

'Pretty please? From the look of your desk I'm guessing you're not run off your feet with exciting assignments?'

'As it's you. But you'll owe me, don't forget.'

Libby is as good as her word, arriving a few minutes before lunchtime on Wednesday, waving a paper bag at me.

'Cheese and pickle, or cheese and salad?'

'I'm not fussed. Just give me five minutes to close up.'

I put the *Closed for lunch* sign on the door, lock it and offer Libby the spare chair.

'What have you found?' I ask her.

'Bad news. Precisely nothing. I scoured the whole of that week's edition and there was nothing remotely of interest. The usual write-ups about the local WI, births, marriages and deaths. Tidehaven was desperate to return to normality after the war. Rationing was still a big problem, though. There were dreadful shortages, and for the families who had lost a breadwinner to the fighting, or maybe their whole house, well it would have been awfully grim.'

The surge of hope I'd felt when Libby arrived immediately dissipates. It's as if I've just been ditched.

'Eat your sandwich,' she says.

'I've lost my appetite.'

'Come on, don't be so easily discouraged. Let's take a look at the article again. Have you got it here?'

I pull the envelope out from under the counter, remove the press cutting and spread it out between us.

'Right, what would Poirot do?' she says.

'I have no idea. The problem with the whole Poirot thing is that it's not real and this is. It's not just frustrating. If Dorothy's life is truly in danger I need to find her and soon.' I push the sandwich away, as the hiccups begin. 'Oh, Bean, give me a break with these blessed hiccups. It's driving me nuts.'

'You need to calm down. Take some deep breaths and we'll approach this in a professional manner.' She winks and points to the glass of water beside me.

'You're right,' I take a sip of water and steady my breathing and the hiccups dissipate. 'We have to assume it's the article that is relevant. Not the date, or the fact that it's in the *Tidehaven Observer*.'

'Yes, good. What else?'

'We have a photo of a group of people in front of the Elmrock Theatre. There was a chess match. Maybe it's to do with that? Perhaps there was some kind of scam, maybe Dorothy witnessed something and now someone is after her?'

'Why wait so long?'

'Maybe she's blackmailing them?'

'Yes, but why wait twenty-five years? It doesn't make sense. But you have triggered a thought,' Libby says. 'If Dorothy was there, maybe she is in this photo. We could be looking right at her.'

I put my duffel bag up on the counter, rifle through it and take out my notebook. Slipped inside the front cover is the photo of Dorothy that Hugh gave me. We study it and compare it to the faces in the press article.

'Waste of time,' I say. 'There are two or three women that could be Dorothy, but their faces are too indistinct and faded now, after all this time.'

'Oh, Libby, do you know, the longer I carry on with this case, the more I feel like I'm on a wild goose chase.'

'*Nil desperandum.*'

'Blimey, I didn't know I had such an intelligent assistant.'

'I loved Latin at school. Every translation was like a puzzle, trying to decipher all those funny words, with their strange endings.'

'Were you good at it?'

'Of course. What about you?'

'Of course,' I say and grin. 'Now, getting back to the matter in hand, what are we going to do next?'

'I have an idea.'

'I always feel slightly nervous when you say that.'

'You'll like this one. We can make a two-pronged attack.'

'Sounds painful?'

'Seriously. I have the details of all the people who wrote in for the nostalgia article. I could visit each of them, explaining that we would like to do an in-depth piece, focusing on their story. I could have the chess article with me and present it to them, in a nonchalant fashion and ask if they remember anything about that day.'

'Nonchalant?'

'I can do nonchalant with the best of them, I'll have you know,' she says, beaming. 'Now, the other prong is you. You can do the same thing in the library van. Have both articles out on the counter, or on the noticeboard and engage people in conversation about them.'

'On what pretext?'

'You'll think of something.'

'Great, thanks for that. Only one problem. We only have one copy of the chess article.'

'Ever heard of photocopying?'

We agree to compare notes after a week.

'You sure your boss won't mind? Won't he wonder what you're up to?' I ask her.

'I'm still in his good books. Sales of the paper went up off the back of the nostalgia article, so I'm on a roll. I need to make the most of it before he changes his mind. But before you dash off, give me your hands.'

'Oh, crikey, not that again.'

I hold out my hands, revealing ten chewed fingernails.

'I've made it my mission to rid you of the disgusting habit, so humour me. Let's make a date and I'll paint them for you. Shall I come to you?'

'Yes, Saturday night, if you're free?'

'Perfect, I'll be there.'

A vague thought is forming in my mind. It's time to come clean with Greg and having Libby there as back up might not be such a bad idea.

Chapter 15

I'm due for an ante-natal check-up, so as soon as I drop the van back to the car park, I make my way to the clinic. A few of the mothers are huddled in a group and as I approach, I realise they have circled around a young woman who has her head down between her knees and is making groaning noises. Before I can say or do anything one of the midwives arrives and eases her way through the group.

'If you could all move back and give Mrs Bertrand some air,' she says.

We step back, but continue watching while the midwife speaks quietly to the woman, rubbing her back.

'Is she going to be alright?' one of the other mothers says. 'It'll be morning sickness I expect. They call it morning sickness, but it grabs you any time of day. I've had it with all of mine, dreadful it is. Makes me wonder why I keep putting myself through it.'

'It's alright for you, you're married so you could go on the pill if you wanted,' another woman in the crowd pipes up. A hush descends, as if an imaginary line has been crossed.

'That'll do,' the midwife says, attempting to take control of a situation that is feeling increasingly uncomfortable. The young woman is now sitting up, still looking peaky and holding her hands across her tummy. As I move away to one of the empty chairs I notice that her ring finger is bare. It would appear Mrs Bertrand is still a Miss, a fact that may have contributed to the flurry of unspoken opinions about the plight of unmarried mothers.

'How long am I going to be plagued with these hiccups?' I ask the midwife, once she has confirmed that everything appears to be in order, as far as Bean is concerned. 'I'm six months into my pregnancy, shouldn't my symptoms have settled down by now? You would have thought my body would be used it after all this time.'

'It doesn't really work like that.' The midwife is young, fresh-faced, possibly a year or two younger than me. She has a calm, confident manner about her and I think about the way life filters each of us in a particular direction. What kind of midwife would I make? How would she be as a librarian? Or a private investigator, come to that.

We chat for a while about breathing techniques.

'You need to be mindful of your diet,' she says. 'Regular meals, but small portions. Little and often is probably the best way forward. And avoid anything spicy, or fizzy drinks.'

'Seems like Bean is a fussy little thing.'

'Bean?'

'Yes, that's what we call it. Makes it easier than saying 'he' or 'she' all the time.'

She looks at me quizzically.

'It started out looking like a kidney bean, or at least that's what the pictures in the textbook reminded me of.'

'Bean, it is then,' she says and smiles. 'Pregnancy can do all sorts of things to your body, some people have a lot of trouble with sickness and so on and others sail through. And there's no saying your next pregnancy will be the same as this one.'

'Don't worry, there's no next pregnancy on the cards.'

'You never know what's around the corner.'

'When you've mapped out your route, that's exactly what you do know. One Bean is fine with me, thanks.'

As I leave the cubicle, I spot Nikki waiting to go in next.

'Shall I wait for you? We could grab a drink afterwards?' I say, as she passes me.

She hesitates and nods. 'Okay, yes, I won't be long.'

After five minutes or so she emerges, frowning.

'Is everything alright? You seem worried,' I say.

'Fine, everything is fine.' Her words and her voice don't match up.

We leave the clinic and walk down to one of our regular pit-stops. As we walk, I chatter about the guidance the midwife has given me, but Nikki says very little, just nodding occasionally in response.

Once inside the café I order two lemonades, temporarily ignoring the midwife's advice about fizzy drinks and we take a seat at a table furthest away from the door. There's a real autumn chill in the air today and I'm grateful for the warmth of the café.

'Are you okay, you seem a bit quiet?' I say.

She looks at me, but doesn't respond.

'You did get my thank you card, didn't you? It was a lovely evening. You're an excellent cook. Greg is still on about your Yorkshires. And the company was great too, in fact, we got on so well with your neighbours, Howard and Joanne, we're planning another get-together with them. They've got a boat, you know, a little fishing boat. I took dad and Charlie out in it and, well, that's another story. Bit of a disastrous day, to be honest.'

As I'm rambling she is looking down at her lemonade, running a finger around the rim of the glass. I pause to take a breath and then she speaks.

'Frank wants to see you,' she says.

'Right. Sorry, how do you mean, he wants to see me?'

'At the police station. He wants to see you in his official capacity as Detective Sergeant. He asked me to ask you next time I saw you.'

'Oh, right.' I'm not sure how to respond and a hundred questions are running around my head. 'I'm surprised he's asked you to speak to me. I thought he was an advocate of not mixing work and home life?'

She gives me a blank look, as though my comment has made her wonder about her husband's motives.

'Is that why you're upset with me? Because of something Frank has said?' I ask her.

'You make it very difficult for us to be friends, Janie.'

'Do I? How do I make it difficult?'

'Frank has to be my priority. He's my husband and whatever you think of him, I love him.'

'Nikki, I have no idea what this is all about. I'm sorry if you feel I've done something wrong, but I thought we agreed to focus on our friendship and not let anything our husbands do or say interfere with that.'

She shakes her head and doesn't reply.

'So, are we still friends?' I ask her.

'Will you go and see Frank?'

'Yes, of course I will. I'll go straight there this evening.'

'Well, that's good. I'm sorry, Janie, but for now I think we need to call a halt to our friendship. Maybe when things settle down again, then...'

'You're speaking in riddles. I don't know what you are hoping will 'settle down' but fine, yes. Whatever you like. If you'd rather not be friends, I'm sad about that, but I respect your decision.'

I pay for the drinks and leave the café before she sees me cry. I can't remember the last time I cried. This is hardly a monumentally difficult experience, so I hold my hand on my midriff and whisper to Bean that he or she needs to take the blame for my over-emotional response. The last time a girl chose to stop speaking to me was when I was thirteen. I can't even remember why we'd fallen out. The injustice I felt then resurfaces now, made worse because I don't even know what I'm meant to have done. Hopefully a visit to Tidehaven Police Station will provide some answers.

When I last visited the police station I was bringing DS Bright news about Zara. This time, though, I've been summoned. I present myself at the front desk and ask to see Detective Sergeant Bright.

'And you are?' the desk officer asks.

'Mrs Janie Juke. He's expecting me. At least, he's asked to see me.'

'Righto, miss. If you'd like to take a seat for a moment, I'll see if he's free.'

After a few moments the desk officer reappears, followed by Frank Bright. He nods a greeting and gestures to me to follow him.

Tidehaven Police Station must have just one interview room, because the room he shows me into is the same room I have sat in on several occasions, during my search for Zara. The room is bare, except for a wooden table and two uncomfortable wooden chairs. The single window casts a dull light and, at a guess, is permanently closed, resulting in an almost suffocating stuffiness. From my previous dealings with Frank, I know he's a smoker, but fortunately this time he has no ashtray in his hand. Someone has recently been smoking in the room, though, as the cloying smell lingers.

'Thank you for coming, Mrs Juke. Do take a seat.' His voice is measured, almost formal.

It's strange to think that the last time we spoke, we were standing looking at a photo of his dead wife. Any softness in his personality I detected then, is not in evidence today.

'How can I help you?' I say.

'I've had a complaint.'

'A complaint?'

'Yes, a complaint about you.'

I hold his gaze, trying to ascertain how the conversation might go from here.

'Can you tell me anything about this complaint? Like who made it?'

'I'm not at liberty to disclose the name of the person making the complaint. But I'm told you've been making a nuisance of yourself, asking questions, following people.'

'Following people? You don't need to tell me who. It's Kenneth Elm, isn't it?'

He stares at me, narrowing his eyes a little, but doesn't respond.

'Can I be open with you, Detective Sergeant?'

'I would appreciate it if you were.'

'Mr Elm has an extremely threatening manner.'

'Has he threatened you?'

'Not in a direct way, no. But he has threatened an acquaintance of mine. In fact, as a result of his interference and bullying, my acquaintance is now very poorly, in hospital.'

'I see. And can you tell me the name of this 'acquaintance'?'

'The thing is,' I continue, ignoring his question, 'my acquaintance was worried he was being followed. So, he asked me to investigate and that's when I came across Mr Elm.'

'You were following the follower?'

'Yes, that's about the size of it.'

'What concerns me, Mrs Juke, is your use of the word 'investigate'. I thought we'd agreed not so long ago that 'investigation' is the job of the police force, not librarians.'

This is a pivotal moment. Do I share what I know with the police, despite Hugh's insistence that the police are not to be involved? DS Bright can throw more resources at the problem than I can drum up, even with Libby's help. However, any police involvement could scare Dorothy even further into hiding. On the other hand, if she is in danger, maybe police protection is exactly what she needs.

'I'm sorry Mr Elm felt he had to approach you,' I say. 'And I'm surprised you involved your wife. As a result, Nikki now feels she can't be friends with me. Or perhaps that was your intention?'

'I'm sure you will agree with me that you have a different way of looking at the world, Mrs Juke. Nikki is a gentle soul, I don't want her upset.'

'You mean you don't want her to make her own choices?'

'As I told you the other evening, I am old-fashioned and my wife and I understand each other. But I haven't asked you here to talk about my wife. You still haven't told me the name of your acquaintance. Please remember, if you have information that may be relevant to a police enquiry, you need to share that information. It's an offence not to disclose...'

'Yes, I know,' I interrupt him, holding my hand out to shake his. 'If that's all Detective Sergeant, I'll be off. I will bear in mind what you've told me though, and if there's anything I feel I need to share with you, then, of course...'

This time, it is his turn to interrupt. 'Mrs Juke, this is not about needing to share, we're not talking about a mother's meeting here. If you are aware of any crime that has been committed, it is for us to investigate, not you. Do you understand?'

'I do, really I do. And I'm grateful to know that I can call on you, should I need to. It's very reassuring.'

'We're not the back-up reserves, you know,' he says, frustration evident in his tone.

'No, of course not,' I say smiling.

I leave the police station more determined than ever to discover what it is that Kenneth Elm is so keen for me not to find out.

Chapter 16

Whenever the weather is damp, the library van chooses not to start. I've told my boss at the Central Library about it an endless number of times and am just encouraged to 'coax' it into action. Some mornings it's all I can do to coax myself into action, so the added problems with my place of work is one thing I can do without. As a result of the coaxing, by the time I arrive at my regular Wednesday parking place in Rockwell Crescent, Mrs Latimer is there waiting for me. She is returning her husband's book.

'He's a fast reader,' I say, as we walk into the van together. 'Let me take my coat off. How is Bobby? Any better? Is he back at school?'

She sighs and remains hovering at the counter.

'You've had quite a walk, why not sit for a while, it's nice to have someone to chat to.'

She nods and looks relieved, unwinding the scarf from around her neck. I pull the spare chair out from behind the counter, unfold it and offer it to her.

'Bobby is much better, thanks,' she says. 'But now it's my mother-in-law, Freda. Edgar, he's my husband, he's that worried about her. She's going downhill fast. He reads to her, you see, that's why he's got through the book so quickly.'

'I'm sorry to hear she's poorly.'

'He's a rock, you know, my Edgar. He does a full day's work, has his tea, then he's straight round to Freda. He makes her supper, settles her down for the night. You wouldn't think it to look at him. Great big lump. But he's as soft as marshmallow inside.'

I silently reprimand myself. Once again, I've made assumptions. Once again, they are wrong.

'Good news about Bobby, though, you must be relieved,' I say.

She nods and her face is transformed with a cheerful smile. 'Do you know, he even joined in the cross-country run the other day. He's got the hang of his inhalers now. As long as he uses one before he sets off, well, he's that happy, being able to join in.'

'Will you be choosing another book for your husband? His mum must be so grateful to have his help and support. Lucky they like the same books,' I say and laugh. 'I've read to my dad for years, but we've always taken it in turns to choose the book. He loves sea-faring adventures, but I'm more into crime.'

She looks at me and raises an eyebrow.

'Crime stories,' I say and we both chuckle, then I point to the noticeboard. 'What did you think of the nostalgia article in the *Observer*? Have you had time to read it yet? I was born after the war, but learning about people's experiences here in Tamarisk Bay, well, it makes you think. It's so easy to take life for granted, isn't it?'

As she stands, I move her chair out of the way, so we can stand side by side in front of the noticeboard. We scan over the article for a few moments, without speaking, then she points to the other press cutting.

'What's this?' she says.

I wait for a while before responding, to give her a moment to inspect the photocopy of the faded sheet.

'It's from the *Tidehaven Observer* just after the war. 1946,' I say.

She moves closer to the noticeboard and peers at the photo.

'Do you know... well, how strange. To think we were talking about her a few moments ago and then, there she is,' she says, pointing at one of the women in the photo.

'That's Freda, that one there.' Her face brightens, it's as though her mother-in-law has suddenly been restored to good health, to youth and vitality. 'Doesn't she look smart? She was always one for making the most of her looks, you know. And she'd never be seen out without a hat. She has some beautiful hat pins, keeps them all in a velvet-lined jewellery box. They might be worth a bob or two, but she'd never sell them. Course, she'll never use them now.'

The smile has fallen from her face, leaving a forlorn expression, her mouth turned down at the edges, accentuating her sallow complexion.

'That's quite a coincidence,' I say. 'Tell you what, I have an idea that might cheer Freda up. I mean, if you agree, if you think she'd be up to it?'

Mrs Latimer appears to be lost in her thoughts for a while and doesn't respond. Then, she shakes herself a little and turns to me. 'What's your idea?'

'Well, it looks as though this was a photo of a happy time for Freda. I could call in, show her the article and chat to her about those days. Maybe bring back happy memories? Of course, she may not like a visit from a stranger, especially if she's not feeling her best,' I say, 'but I'd love to meet her, she sounds like a lovely lady.'

'That's a kind thought. She doesn't get to see many people now, just me and Edgar and Bobby. A couple of neighbours pop in to keep an eye on her, and she has the odd friend still alive, but it's not the same as when she was young. She was involved in everything, helping out at the school, running WI meetings, there wasn't a day went by when she wasn't busy. Edgar often had to make his own tea after school. Mind you, I'm not complaining, at least it means he knows how to cook. Not like some men.'

'You're right there,' I say, recalling the day, not so long ago, when I arrived home to find Greg toasting a frozen fish finger under the grill. 'How about you chat to your husband and let me know? Any evening is fine with me, or a weekend, if that's better. Maybe she'll be less tired if I call in the daytime?'

Two days later I am walking up the front path of 22 Wilmington Avenue, with the chess article tucked safely into my notebook. There's not much I could prepare by way of questions, as I have no idea what Freda will remember about that time, if indeed she'll remember anything. It's a bitterly cold day and yet I have sweaty palms. Just as well I didn't bother wearing gloves.

Mrs Latimer answers the door and beckons me in. We walk down the hall into the kitchen. There is an air of quiet about the house and I am loath to disturb it. Once we're in the kitchen I notice Bobby sitting at the kitchen table, with his head bent over a book.

'Hello there, Bobby, how are you?'

'Very well, thank you, Mrs Juke,' he says, immediately returning his gaze to his book.

'His dad needs some time to himself. Bobby understands, he's a good boy,' his mum says, ruffling her son's hair. 'There's a football match up at the Pilot Field today, so Edgar will wander up there. I've never understood it myself, standing around in the freezing cold, or the pouring rain, watching men kick a ball around.'

'I'm with you, it's nonsensical. But I guess we're all different,' I say and smile.

'Would you like a cup of tea?' She fills the kettle and puts it on the gas.

'I'm fine, really, just a glass of water, if that's okay? How is Freda today?'

'She's dozing at the moment, but she enjoys a hot drink around now, so when we take it through I'll wake her and then you can have a chat.'

'It's a shame to wake her, if she's resting?'

'No, it's best she doesn't sleep too long in the day, otherwise she has bad nights. You sure you won't have a cuppa? I don't know where I'd be without tea, it's my salvation. Everything looks better after a cup of tea, that's what my mum used to say to us when we were growing up.'

I smile and imagine a conversation I may have with Bean one day on the benefits of tea.

Once the kettle boils she fills the teapot, takes two of the delicate china cups and saucers from the kitchen dresser, together with matching milk jug and sugar bowl and lays it all out on a tray.

'This tea set has been in the Latimer family for generations, so Edgar told me. I'm terrified in case I drop a saucer or chip a cup when I do the washing up. But Freda loves to see it being used, it gives her pleasure. Happy memories, I suppose.'

I follow Mrs Latimer out of the kitchen. She explains that since Freda's health has declined Edgar decided to convert the sitting room into a bedroom for her. The door is pushed open and we walk into a room that is in darkness, with the curtains drawn. Setting the tea tray down on the sideboard, which is now doubling up as a dressing table, she moves over to the window and pulls back the heavy, damask curtains. Milky sunlight floods the room.

Freda looks so peaceful. She is completely still, turned to one side, with the blankets and bedspread tucked right up to her chin. Wisps of silver grey hair are stuck to the side of her face. A heavy scent of violets fills the air.

Mrs Latimer moves over to the bed and lays a hand gently on Freda's shoulder. 'Wake up now, Freda, there's a visitor to see you.'

For a few moments there is no response or movement, then I notice the bedcovers move, as she stretches her legs out and wriggles a little.

'I'm going to pour you a nice cup of tea, then we'll get you sat up,' Mrs Latimer says.

'I can sit myself up, you know, Ethel. I'm not a complete invalid,' Freda says, her voice still heavy with sleep.

After a bit more wriggling and repositioning of pillows she is sitting upright, sipping her tea. Mrs Latimer pulls a chair over to the bedside and gestures for me to sit down.

'Mum, this is Janie. Do you remember, we told you she'd be visiting? Janie runs the mobile library here in Tamarisk Bay.'

Freda looks at me. 'So sad about your father,' she says.

'Do you know my dad?' I'm annoyed with myself for not realising. This is Tamarisk Bay, of course, she would know him. He's lived in the town all his life, as has Freda, I'm guessing.

'He's doing incredibly well,' I say. 'He's a brilliant physiotherapist, a real natural.'

She smiles and nods her head. 'He was a bright lad, could have done anything he put his mind to. If the blessed war hadn't come along...' She pauses and closes her eyes for a moment, as if lost in a private reverie.

Freda's daughter-in-law glances across at me, then points to my duffel bag.

'Mum,' she says, 'Janie has something to show you. I bet you'll be surprised when you see it.'

Freda opens her eyes and watches me as I retrieve my notebook and remove the press article. Taking one of the books from the bedside table I lay the article on top, flatten it out and hand it to Freda.

'What's this?' she says. 'Ethel, get my spectacles, will you?'

Putting her spectacles on, she peers at the sheet of paper. 'We need more light. Why is it always so dull in here?' she says, a touch of irritation in her voice.

Ethel turns the bedside lamp on and angles it towards the bed. It casts a yellow light over the paper, making the photo appear more faded than ever.

'Your daughter-in-law thought she recognised you in the photo,' I say. 'It was twenty-five years ago, so you might not remember it after all this time.'

Freda looks up at me and then back down at the article. She shifts herself slightly so that she is sitting more upright. 'Of course,' she says. 'The photo. I'd forgotten the chess match.'

'It must have been a big occasion.'

'You were involved in all sorts of groups and committees back then, weren't you mum?' Ethel says. 'I remember you telling me about a group who organised the twinning of Tidehaven with Dordrecht back in the fifties.'

Ethel turns to me to explain, 'Twinning of towns was a big thing, people saw it as a way to bring countries together after the war had divided so much of Europe.'

Freda nods her head slowly, her eyes now much brighter, a pink glow coming into her cheeks to lighten the pallor of her skin.

'You must have had the chance to meet some interesting people,' I say, 'I'm guessing there were foreign visitors, dignitaries? Everyone is dressed so smartly. You look so glamorous, I love that hat of yours.'

Then she smiles. 'Yes, my dear. Everyone was dressed smartly, but here's a lesson for you, don't always believe what you see.'

She lays her head back against the pillow and closes her eyes. Ethel looks at me and I am wondering if that is all Freda plans to share with us. I throw a questioning glance at Ethel and turn towards the door, wondering if this is when I should leave, but then I hear Freda's voice.

'The chess match was overshadowed by the other event that took place that day,' she says.

'Another event?' I ask her.

'Yes, my dear,' she says. 'I remember it well. It was the one and only time I've ever been slapped.'

Ethel and I glance at each other and then at Freda, who now has her eyes open and a mischievous smile on her face.

'What do you mean, mum? Are you getting your words mixed up?'

'I'm not getting anything mixed up,' her voice is strong now, almost indignant. 'I might have forgotten the chess match, but my memory of everything that happened afterwards is as sharp as though it was yesterday. Not surprising, is it?'

'But you've never mentioned it before, mum. Edgar's never said.'

'That's because he doesn't know. No-one knew, except my Arthur. I told him as soon as I got home that day and he went straight round to the house. There was a terrible row, by all accounts. The neighbours came out onto the street to see what was going on.'

'Was there a fight? Did Arthur end up getting hurt?' Ethel asks.

'No, not a bit of it. All Arthur could do was shout. After all, he would never have lifted his hand to a woman.'

'A woman?' Ethel's voice is raised in disbelief.

'That's right. The woman who hit me, she's standing there right next to me in the photo. Her name is Dorothy. Dorothy Elm.'

Chapter 17

At last I have positive news of sorts to report to Libby when we meet at *Jefferson's,* as arranged. With coffees ordered we sit at our favourite table, away from the juke box. Before I can open my mouth, she waves her hand at me.

'No, me first,' she says. 'I've been busy. I've interviewed five people and not a single one of them remembers the chess event. So, that's all quite hopeless. But...' she pauses for effect.

'But what?' I say, impatiently.

'One of the chaps I interviewed knows Kenneth Elm. Went to school with him, in fact.'

'Oh right. So how did that crop up? The Kenneth Elm connection?'

She wriggles in her seat. 'Well,' she says, biting her bottom lip, 'I happened to mention that we were trying to pin down the names of the people in the photo and we thought one of them might have been called Dorothy Elm. And that's when he told me about Kenneth.'

'I think that's what they call 'leading the witness'.

She smiles and continues. 'It's fascinating because this chap said that when they were at school together Kenneth regularly came to school with holes in his shoes, or worse. He wore wellingtons in summer. Basically, the family were really poor.'

'Well, we know that from what Phyllis told me. The father lost his job and the mother was cleaning and taking in laundry. It must have been so hard for them all. But how is that relevant?'

'It's what happened after that is relevant, or could be. The chap told me that Dorothy left Tamarisk Bay during the war and Kenneth stayed behind.

'Yes, we know that too. Kenneth would have been too young to fight and Dorothy became a land girl. That's when she met Hugh.'

'Yes, but when she came back, everything changed.'

'Changed? In what way? Did he say?'

'He just said there were rumours. I pushed him as hard as I could, but he wouldn't say another word. He completely clammed up on me.'

'So, not exactly a help,' I say, failing to disguise my irritability.

'Don't get mad at me. I've done you a favour. At least I've found out something.'

'Sorry, I'm not mad at you. It's great, really it is. It's just that we get close to a useful clue and then come up against a blank wall again.'

'What about you?' she says. 'Did you find out anything from your customers?'

'Let's have another coffee and I'll tell you.'

By the time we have finished our drinks I have told her about Freda and her memorable encounter with Dorothy Elm.

'Did she explain why Dorothy slapped her?'

'It was difficult. She's such a sweet lady, I felt bad asking her about it. She started to get quite distressed.'

'I bet she did. Being reminded that someone hit you would be incredibly upsetting.'

'She wasn't teary or anything like that, just the opposite. She was indignant, saying the thought of *"that woman"* made her want to jump out of bed and track her down. In fact, it was inspiring to see her so full of attitude. That's how I want to be when I'm old.'

'Poor Greg if he's got that to look forward to,' Libby says, grinning.

'Ah, yes, well maybe we'll have attitude together.'

140

'Then poor Bean. Maybe he or she will take a ten-pound passage to Australia to get away from you both. But let's not drift off the subject, what else did Freda say?'

'Not a lot more. Her daughter-in-law, Ethel, was concerned we'd disturbed her. It's not good for her to get upset. Ever since Freda had a stroke, well, you can imagine.'

'Ah, so not a good plan then.'

'Exactly.'

'Did you find out anything else?'

'I asked her if Dorothy still lived in Tidehaven, which is where she was when Freda had her run in with her.'

'Tidehaven is a big place and 1946 was a long time ago.'

'It's all we have to go on right now. We know Kenneth is still in touch with Dorothy and he is our only lead. He's bound to visit her at some point. How about we follow him?'

'You make it sound so simple. You've forgotten two small things. First up we both have jobs, which means we can't go off at a moment's notice. Secondly, you have been warned to stay away from Kenneth by the police.'

'Ah, yes,' I say, nodding.

'That's quite serious, Janie. You don't want to have your baby in prison.'

I smile as I think back to a similar conversation I had with Greg during my search for Zara. 'We will be really careful. We don't need to get too close. We only need to see the house he goes into from a distance. I might finally get to use my camera.'

'And then what?'

'Then we wait until he leaves and knock on the door.'

'So, you plan to sit outside the vets every evening, in the hope he decides to visit his sister? I'm sure Greg would love that. I have a feeling you would run out of excuses pretty soon.'

I take my notebook out of my duffel bag, for the want of something to do, while I mull over the problem.

'Here's a thing,' I say, as I flick through my most recent pages of notes. 'Let's consider Hugh and Dorothy. Hugh was a war hero of sorts, a pilot, prepared to undertake dangerous missions. But Kenneth says he's a liar. Dorothy must have been courageous too, taking on tough farm work and then risking her life trying to help the French resistance. And yet, from what Freda says, Dorothy is not a very nice person. You don't go around hitting people if you're a nice person, do you?'

The images that poor Freda has conjured up in my mind remind me of Owen's revelations during my search for Zara. The more I learn about people, the more complex they appear. I guess some people manage to keep their anger in check and others have no compunction about letting loose. Then there are others who appear not to have an angry bone in their body, like my dad, for example. But who knows what deep thoughts may lie festering, until one day the cap of the volcano bursts open and they all come tumbling out.

'We also have the chap I spoke to,' Libby says, bringing me back to the present. 'Mr Task his name is. He suggested there were rumours about the Elm family.'

'The crux of the problem is that both the people we are dealing with - Hugh and Dorothy - have things to hide. Plus, if they both worked with the SOE they will be experts at keeping secrets.'

Libby fidgets on her seat, taking the sugar bowl from the centre of the table and moving it from side to side.

'Playing chess?' I say.

'It is a bit like chess, isn't it? Trying to second guess the other person's next move. Freda says Dorothy was there in Tidehaven for the chess match, but we still don't know if Dorothy stayed in Tidehaven. She may have moved away by now. I hate to say this, Janie, but I think we're wasting our time. I suggest you tell Hugh what you've found out so far and let him do what he will with it.'

'You keep telling me to drop it, but like I said before, Hugh is too ill to do anything.'

'Well, that's not really your problem, is it?'

Libby is right, there are too many questions left unanswered in my notebook. Hugh hasn't told me the whole truth about Dorothy, I'm sure of it.

On my next day with dad I talk it through with him.

'You like to make life difficult for yourself, don't you?' he says.

'Any ideas about what I could do next? Other than abandoning the whole thing?'

We are in the kitchen, Charlie is sitting beside dad, with his head on dad's knee.

'It's a shame you're not a sniffer dog, Charlie,' I say, rubbing his head.

'What would you want him to sniff?'

'The truth of the situation. Right now, it feels as though I'm trying to knit a complicated Arran sweater without a pattern, using the wrong sized needles.'

'You've never knitted in your life,' dad says and smiles. 'Do what you did with Zara, go back to basics.'

'I thought we'd done that with Libby's nostalgia article. I thought looking into the past would help to make the present day a bit clearer.'

'Do you think Freda will say any more about the slapping incident?'

'I can't push her on it, she's very frail. It's not fair to ask her to remember such an upsetting event.'

'And you say Freda was involved at the school? Is that your old school? Grosvenor Grammar, where Phyllis taught?'

As I jump up, Charlie lifts his head from dad's knee and looks at me.

'You are an absolute marvel,' I say, as I bend down to give dad a hug.

'Am I?' he says, smiling. Charlie stands beside us, looking expectantly.

'No, Charlie, this does not mean an early walk. It means that your master here has once again guided this rookie detective down the correct path.'

'Pleased to be of service,' dad says, putting his hand out to rest on Charlie's head. 'Keep me posted?'

'Of course. I'll go and see Phyllis right now, if that's okay with you boss?'

'Done all your jobs for the day?'

'Yep.'

'Off you go then. I hope she can help. But Janie, if she can't, you might need to think seriously about letting this one go.'

Now that the afternoons are getting shorter and the evenings longer, I'm certain I'll find Phyllis at home, either baking in a warm kitchen, or reading in front of the fire. She takes a few moments to answer the door and when she does, she looks a little flustered.

'Ah, it's you,' she says. 'Come in, come in.'

I follow her through to the kitchen and notice she is limping.

'Everything okay?' I ask her.

She sits down on one of the kitchen chairs and sighs.

'Hey, that's not like you. What's the problem?'

'Just a stupid moment. I was down the bottom of the garden, moving a few of the pots around. It's way past the time when I should have got my bulbs in. I must have twisted awkwardly and I felt my ankle give way.'

'Ouch,' I say, putting my hand on her shoulder. 'Have you tried a cold compress? Or soaking in vinegar? That's supposed to help. Do you want me to take a look?'

'I should be offering you a cup of something,' she says, lifting her leg up a little, revealing a swollen ankle.

'Don't even think about it. Tell you what, why not go and put your leg up on the settee to rest it and I'll fix us something hot to drink.'

She nods, gets up and slowly makes her way through to the sitting room. A while later, once the kettle has boiled, I go through to join her, taking a tray with drinks, together with the biscuit barrel.

'I've taken the liberty,' I say, offering her a biscuit. 'Something sweet to help with the shock, or the pain, or both.'

I sit in the armchair beside her and for a while we sip our drinks in silence.

'Tell me something interesting to take my mind off this wretched ankle,' she says. 'How is your case going?'

'Well, funny you should ask,' I say, smirking.

'Have you come to quiz me again? I'm not sure what else I can tell you about the Elm boy.'

'It's someone else this time. Do you remember Freda Latimer?'

'Remember her? We're still friends. Such a lovely lady, it's a real shame she's become so frail. She was a veritable powerhouse when she was younger.'

145

'She mentioned that she helped out at the school. I don't remember her, so it wasn't during my time at Grosvenor?'

'No, it was much earlier. Back in the fifties. She was a school governor. I don't know how she found time to do all that she did. You think of a committee back then and Freda Latimer was involved in one way or another. Like I say, a veritable powerhouse.'

'She's told me about a run-in with Dorothy Elm.'

'A run-in? Can you be a bit more specific?'

'Well, she's alleging that Dorothy slapped her.'

'Are you sure? Freda was a fiery sort in her heyday, I can't imagine anyone getting one over on her.'

'So, she's never mentioned the incident to you? It's not something you remember?'

I take my notebook out and remove the press cutting, passing it over to Phyllis to look at. 'It happened the day this photo was taken. At least that's Freda's memory of it.'

Phyllis examines the newspaper cutting, reading through the short article. 'It certainly looks like Freda there, although the photo is very faded. And you say that's Dorothy standing next to her? '

'Well, it's possible Freda is confused. It was a long time ago, after all.'

'Do you want me to see what I can find out? I could drop in on Freda and talk to her about it?'

'I don't think you should be going anywhere with that dodgy ankle. R and R is what I am prescribing.'

'And when have you known me to put my feet up? You've got me intrigued now. I see what Libby means about this amateur sleuthing lark, it's quite addictive, isn't it?'

'Leave it with me, I'm the one being paid, after all.'

Chapter 18

Hugh is to be discharged from hospital on Thursday.

'The doctor says he is a little better,' Mrs Summer says when she calls into the library to let me know. 'No oxygen now. That is good. Very good.'

'I'm so pleased to hear it. Will he be able to manage the stairs alright?' Hugh's room at number 22 is up two flights of steep stairs of the Victorian property.

'Yes, slowly, slowly,' she says. 'He rings me from the hospital. "*Mrs Summer*," he says, "*may I come back?*" Of course, I say, your room is waiting for you.'

'Well, I'm sure he'll be relieved. I'll call in if that's alright. Later in the afternoon, let him settle first.'

'Yes, we can all have tea together,' she says, looking delighted with the thought of an impromptu tea party.

Hugh's lodgings are at the far end of First Avenue. Each of the houses have small front gardens, and even smaller walled courtyards at the rear. But as they border the edge of Maze Gardens they benefit from a charming outlook. Even though the trees are almost bare now, there is a beauty in their starkness and today the sky is clear and the sun is bright, after an early morning frost. Thinking about the cold months ahead, my mind turns to Greg. This will be his first winter with the building firm. The weather won't bother him, after all, before joining Mowbray's he was a window cleaner, where our British climate presented its own problems. But as a brickie, or at least a bricklayer's apprentice, I wonder what happens when it's too cold to lay bricks. Will he still get paid? Maybe any money I get from Hugh should be ferreted away into a snowy day fund, just in case.

I arrive at the Summer household with a packet of jam tarts nestled inside my duffel bag, adjacent to my notebook. I'm hoping the former won't turn the latter into a sticky mess.

Mrs Summer invites me through to her sitting room, where Hugh is nestled in an armchair close to the coal fire, with a rug around his knees.

'Well, you look warm and cosy there,' I say.

'Mrs Juke, you sit here,' she points to an armchair next to Hugh, 'and I will get the tea.'

'Oh, I've brought these,' I say, digging into my bag to retrieve the jam tarts.

'Very kind,' she says.

'Um, may I have coffee? For some strange reason, since I've been pregnant, I haven't been able to drink tea. Silly, I know.'

'Not silly. I don't understand how you English can drink tea with milk. I drink it with lemon, but it was many years before I get used to the taste. Until then, only water. I drink always water,' she says, holding her hands up with an expression of despair.

'Ah, I thought I could detect an accent, Mrs Summer. Where were you born?'

'In Puglia, the south of Italy. Please call me Rosetta.'

'How wonderful and you met your husband in Italy?'

'Yes, in the war. We fall in love and then I come here and he dies, leaving me to your cold English winters.'

I give her a half smile, then turn to see how Hugh is coping with this mention of dying. I'm guessing it's not the upbeat conversation a doctor would recommend for a recuperating patient.

'You're right about the cold winters,' Hugh says quietly, 'although it's a wonderful excuse for a coal fire.'

'I go to make the tea,' Rosetta says.

I sit next to Hugh and look intently at him.

'Now,' I say, 'how are you? You're looking better than the last time I saw you.'

'Hospitals don't encourage wellness. It's difficult to look healthy when you're surrounded by sick people,' he says and smiles. He is still talking slowly, managing small breaths in-between each word. 'Do you have any news for me?'

I find myself faced with the same dilemma as I did when Hugh was in hospital. I need to choose my words carefully, ensuring I won't upset him in any way and aggravate his condition. Before I can reply, Rosetta comes back into the room with a tray laden with a teapot, a coffee pot and my jam tarts, set out on a delicate china plate. Interspersed with the tarts are assorted biscuits, which she now offers to Hugh and me before pouring our drinks.

'Milk, sugar?' she asks.

Hugh and I speak at once, which makes us all laugh, reducing the tension in the room. Now that Rosetta is sitting with us, I'm wondering how much of a conversation I can have with Hugh. I'm certain he won't want her to know about the case he has tasked me with.

'Would you like to return to Italy?' I ask Rosetta.

'One day, perhaps,' she replies, but she seems loath to say anything more.

'Has the doctor advised you to stay indoors, Hugh?' I say. 'I'm sure the cold winds won't help. It's freezing out there today.'

He smiles and nods.

'Was your husband from Tamarisk Bay, Rosetta? Is that why you settled here?'

'Yes, not far away. His family live in Tidehaven. But we like this house, this area. It is quieter than Tidehaven. I like the quiet.'

'Are you still in touch with his family?' I ask, realising that what started out as an attempt at small talk, now sounds like an interrogation.

'Yes, I go sometimes. His mother, she is very kind to me. His father too. He helps me with my English. Excuse me please. I must look to the supper. I have a chicken in the oven. Mr Furness likes chicken,' she says and swiftly leaves the room. I feel like breathing a sigh of relief, but suppress it.

Hugh turns to me, his expression is tense. 'Did you have anything to tell me? About Dorothy?'

'I do have a little bit more information. It would appear Dorothy was living in Tidehaven after the war. There's no certainty she's still there, but it's possible.'

'Ah,' he says. 'Yes, that would make sense.'

'I've also spoken to a lady who knew Dorothy. A Mrs Freda Latimer. Does that name mean anything to you?'

He shakes his head.

'Can I ask you something, Hugh?'

He nods and I pause while I attempt to frame the question in the least antagonistic way.

'You had a conversation with Kenneth Elm, when you were in hospital.'

He nods again.

'The conversation upset you, quite a lot. Are you able to share any of it with me? Did it concern Dorothy?'

'I'd rather not say.'

'The thing is, Hugh...' I pause. 'There are some gaps in the information you've given me about Dorothy.'

I watch him and monitor his breathing, holding my own breath to see if I have already gone too far, said too much. 'I know you're concerned she's in danger,' I continue, 'but you haven't been specific about what that danger is. From conversations I've had with various people concerning the

150

Elm family, well, there are rumours, skeletons in the cupboard, so to speak. Can you throw any light on the rumours? And the press cutting, the one you deposited in the left luggage depot. What relevance does it have?'

Before he can reply, the door opens and Rosetta joins us again.

'I have learned to do the English roast. I think I am quite good at it.' She smiles and starts to clear away our cups and plates.

'Yes, you are an excellent cook, I can vouch for that,' says Hugh. 'I have thoroughly enjoyed all the meals I have had since I arrived. Perhaps one day you would cook an Italian supper?'

'I think English people do not like Italian food. You like your vegetables soft, all covered with sauce.'

'Gravy?' I ask and she nods.

'I would love to try some of your Italian cooking,' Hugh says.

'I'm with Hugh, real Italian food by a real Italian cook, now that would be a treat.'

'Then you must come too, with your husband. I make *spaghetti all'amatriciana e insalata tricolore*' she says, flourishing her hands in the air.

'Well, that sounds wonderful, but now I should go and leave Hugh to rest,' I say.

'I'll speak to you again,' Hugh says, pointedly, directing his gaze at me.

'Yes, of course. And thank you Rosetta, for the coffee. I'll see you again soon.'

If I was a child I would tip my toybox over and fling my toys around the room in frustration. I'm back at my starting point. I know a little more about Dorothy, a little more about Hugh. But nothing that will lead me to a solution. I'm a good librarian. Perhaps I will heed everyone's advice and leave it at that.

It's Friday and when Mrs Latimer walks through the door I'm surprised. Framlington Road is further for her to walk. Monday is her usual library day, when I'm parked on Milburn Avenue, just around the corner from her house.

'I haven't come about books,' she says, presenting herself at the counter. Her face is flushed, as though she's been running. But the thought of Ethel Latimer running makes me think of a Great Dane trying to ride a bicycle, out and out incompatibility.

'Take a moment,' I say. 'Did you want to sit for a minute, have some water? You look a little hot.'

She takes me up on my offer, plopping herself down on the wooden chair I've unfolded for her. Each day I bring two flasks with me from home, one with hot water and the other with cold. I pour her a glass of cold water and wait for her to catch her breath.

'I didn't want to leave it too long to let you know,' she says. 'I had the feeling that when you showed Freda that newspaper article, well, it was important, wasn't it? What she told you about her run in with that woman; I could tell from your face, you were shocked, weren't you?'

'A little surprised, maybe,' I say.

'I was too. It's the first time I've ever heard mention of it. It was good of you not to push her for any more information.'

'I wouldn't want to upset her. She's a really charming lady, it's a shame she's not in better health. It must be difficult for your husband, he must worry.'

Ethel takes a handkerchief from her handbag and wipes her face.

'I worry. About Arthur, about Freda and then there's Bobby.'

'And who worries about you?' I say, putting my hand on her shoulder.

'Oh, I'm alright, just having a bad day.'

'I hadn't realised that Phyllis Frobisher is friends with your mother-in-law. She mentioned it to me the other day. It turns out they've been friends since way back, when Freda was a school governor.'

She nods. 'That's what I wanted to tell you. Phyllis called in to see Freda. I was there with Bobby, Arthur had to pick up a prescription from the doctor's, so I said we'd wait there with Freda. Then Phyllis turned up and I left them to chat. I was fussing around in the kitchen and I didn't mean to eavesdrop, but I heard the name Dorothy Elm and, well, I'll admit I was curious.'

'Did you find out what it was all about, why Freda and Dorothy had their falling out?'

'I couldn't make much sense of it, to be honest with you. But if I tell you what I heard, well perhaps it will mean something to you.'

I hold my breath in anticipation.

'"*I couldn't leave it alone, after all that their poor mother went through. She would have turned in her grave.*" That's what Freda said.'

'Couldn't leave what alone?'

'I don't know, but I do know that whatever it was, Freda is still upset about it now, all these years later.'

'And she said this to Phyllis?'

Ethel nods, then stands up and hands me her empty glass. 'You are close friends with Phyllis, maybe she can help throw more light on it? I must go now, thank you for the water.'

Perhaps my next visit to Phyllis will help me jump the next hurdle, or at least get me off the starting blocks. I'm starting to think that Phyllis and Libby deserve at least half of any money Hugh has given me to solve this case.

Chapter 19

Aside from some food shopping, Greg and I are enjoying a quiet Saturday.

'Cheese on toast for lunch,' I say, putting the last of the fruit into the bowl.

'Perfect. Did I tell you that dad has offered to help me decorate Bean's room? If we choose the wallpaper and paint, then he'll come over evenings and weekends. It shouldn't take us long if there's two of us.'

'That's really kind and a good idea to get it done early. It'll mean Bean won't have to put up with the smell of fresh paint for the first few weeks of its life. Crikey, just imagine, a pretty nursery instead of an untidy box room. It'll inspire me to sort out all those old books and photos. I've got stuff in there from schooldays.'

'Let me guess, old school reports suggesting you should 'concentrate more'?'

'I think I was a bit of a dreamer. What about yours then? I bet you were only happy when you were outside kicking a ball around?'

'I couldn't stand being cooped up in a classroom.'

'George Best probably said the same thing and he's done alright for himself. By the way, I meant to say, Libby's calling in this evening, if that's okay?'

'Fine with me.'

'You're not going to the pub, are you?'

'I hadn't planned to, no. Why? Do you want me out of the way, so you girls can natter?'

'No, quite the reverse. She's coming to do my nails. She reckons she can cure me of nailbiting by painting them for me. I'm not convinced, but it's worth a go.'

'I've been meaning to ask you about that. I watch you sometimes and I'm sure you don't even realise you're doing it. When we're relaxing in the evening, or at least when I'm relaxing, there you are chewing away. Is everything okay?'

'How do you mean?'

'With Bean, with your dad?'

'Yes.' I feel a flutter inside me that has nothing to do with Bean. 'There is something though.' I pause, acutely aware he is gazing at my face, trying to read my expression. 'I need to tell you something, but I don't want you to be angry.'

He moves towards me and takes my hand.

'Come on, let's sit down. I'm guessing this has something to do with you being late home most days? Has Libby roped you into some hare-brained scheme?'

'Libby is involved, yes,' I hesitate, struggling to find the best way to explain. 'The thing is, well, I've taken on a case.'

'God, Janie, please don't tell me you're off on another one-woman mission to save some unfortunate stranger.'

'No, it's not one woman this time. I've enlisted help. Libby and Phyllis are helping me, well, Libby mostly.' I pause, realising how pathetic my excuses sound. 'I'm sorry I haven't told you before. I know you worry, but you must realise I would never put Bean at risk. It's just that...'

'It's just what?' he interrupts. 'I'm your husband, Janie. Have you forgotten that? I thought we were partners.'

'We are partners, of course we are. I'll try to explain, but to be honest I'm not even sure I understand it myself.'

'Not a great start, then,' he says, his voice heavy with despair.

'I love being married to you and I'm incredibly excited about being a mum. My job at the library gives me a chance to chat to people and surround myself with books and, of course, I treasure my days with dad. But it's not enough for me.'

'You should be grateful for what you've got.'

'I am. But you know how much I love the idea of investigating crime. Agatha Christie and Poirot have been in my blood since forever. It's like trying to solve the best possible puzzle, one where you get to add pieces, move them around and then, if you're lucky, eventually they all fit together and you have a solution.'

'Buy a jigsaw then,' he says.

'It's not only that I love doing it,' I continue, ignoring his sarcasm, 'it's that I'm good at it. So good, in fact, that someone is prepared to pay me.'

I study his expression, which is a mixture of shock and admiration.

'Is that legal? You taking money for services rendered? Is there some kind of written agreement?'

'I don't know if it's legal,' I say, waiting for him to assimilate the information.

'I understand you're ambitious and that's great,' he says. 'I am too, in case you hadn't noticed. But I choose to stay within the law.'

'That's why we make a good pair.'

'Why? Because I'm law-abiding and you're not?'

'No, silly, because we're both ambitious. I'm wrong not to have told you about this case, I know that now. I was scared you would try to stop me.'

'I would have,' he says, a softness returning to his voice.

'Okay, so how about I bring you up to date. I'll tell you about the case so far and then we should make a pact.'

'What kind of pact?'

'I promise to share everything with you from now on.'

'And what do I have to do in return?' he says, a smile starting to creep across his face.

'Ironing or hoovering, take your pick,' I say, standing and holding my arms out to him. 'How about a hug to start though?'

He gets up, wraps his arms around me and pulls me close.

'My wife, a private investigator. Blimey, not sure what the lads at work will make of that.'

'Best not to tell anyone,' I say a little too sharply, before realising he's teasing me.

'Mum's the word,' he says, planting a kiss firmly on my lips. 'Have you thought any more about my dog idea?'

'Yes and no.'

'Well I have. I reckon we should wait until Bean is here and all settled in and then decide how we feel about it. How does that sound?'

'Perfect.'

By the time Libby arrives in the evening I have brought Greg up to date with my search for Dorothy.

'Any thoughts gratefully received,' I say, just before the doorbell rings announcing Libby's arrival.

'Your manicurist, at your disposal, madam,' she says, handing me a cosmetic bag. 'Five colours to choose from, from the most delicate pink, through to the most vampish red. Take your pick.'

'Maybe I'll try the lot,' I say, grinning, 'one on each finger, what do you think?'

'Could be overkill, but you're the boss.'

'In more ways than one, I hear,' Greg says, coming into the hallway.

Libby gives me a quizzical glance, before turning to greet Greg.

'It's okay, I've told him everything. In fact, I was about to ask him to join our investigating team, if that's alright with you? In an advisory capacity only, of course.'

'Er, no, you're okay,' Greg says. 'I don't mind being your sounding board, but I'm not really into racing around chasing people.'

'Don't tell me, you'd rather be in the pub,' Libby says, winking at him.

On the first of December each year I go up into the loft at dad's house and bring down three boxes of Christmas decorations. Each bauble and piece of tinsel is carefully unwrapped and laid out on the dining room table. I select each piece and work my way around the house, bringing festive cheer to every room, even the bathroom. The first year after dad lost his sight, I waited to see what might change. I was coming up for six years old and Christmas was my favourite time of the year. But even then, I realised how inappropriate it was to have a celebration when something so traumatic had happened to the person who was at the centre of my universe.

Mum had already left and Jessica had moved in. I never found out whose idea it was, but I recall being asked to hold the ladder while Jessica went up into the loft to bring down the decorations. It was a Sunday and the three of us had enjoyed a cooked breakfast. As soon as the table was cleared and the washing up was done, dad sat in the only armchair we had in the dining room and Jessica and I emptied the boxes of decorations onto the table. We took it in turns to describe each item in great detail and then it was up to dad to suggest where it would look best. It was as though we were the pupils and dad was our teacher, guiding us to create the most perfect Christmas wonderland, when all he could see was in his mind's eye.

Every year since then I have followed the same routine. Most of the decorations are the same ones I've handled for nearly twenty years, but I still describe them to dad and he still listens attentively. From time to time I have added to our Christmas collection, replacing a broken bauble, or a tattered piece of tinsel. But the fairy that sits on top of the tree has worn well, her dress a little yellowed with age, but her wings still strong and resilient.

With the house looking its Christmas best, dad and I chat for a while about Jessica's forthcoming arrival. There are so many preparations to make I write out three separate lists: *Menus*; *Food shopping*; *Presents*. Dad makes suggestions, interspersed with the occasional reminder, such as *'don't forget Charlie,'* or *'we'll need to air the bedding'*. The time flies by and suddenly it's time for me to leave.

'If you think of anything else, tell me next time,' I say, grabbing my jacket and donning my woolly hat. Among the Christmas goodies retrieved from the loft, I came across a red woollen hat, with a huge pom-pom sewn into its crown. I must have dropped it into one of the boxes when I put the decorations away last January, but I have no memory of it. It's like finding a forgotten friend.

Before I am able to see Phyllis again, Rosetta Summer calls into the library with a note from Hugh.

'Don't forget I will cook, for you and your husband,' she says, handing me an envelope.

'Thank you, yes, that would be something special to look forward to. I'll chat to Greg and we'll come up with some dates.'

'Mr Furness, he gives me this to give to you. He writes, all day he writes. I give him the notepaper my husband left in his desk. My husband too, he loves to write.'

Loved, I think to myself, looking at her forlorn face.

'Does it need a reply? Should I read it straightaway?' I ask her.

'No, it is long, I think. Many pages.' She shakes my hand and goes to embrace me. 'Your baby, when will it arrive?'

'Oh, not for a few months yet. You wouldn't think so to see the size of me, though,' I say, rubbing my hand over my midriff and chuckling.

'A boy, perhaps?'

'Well, it will be one or the other,' I say, realising immediately that Rosetta is unlikely to understand my sense of humour.

'I go now. Shopping to do, for Mr Furness,' she says, looking pleased at the thought of having someone to look after.

'Thank you, it's kind of you to come all this way. Tell Hugh I'll read his letter and I'll be in touch again soon.'

I have the van to myself, so I settle down with a glass of hot water to sip and open the envelope. Rosetta is right, there are several sheets of paper with Hugh's neat writing filling both sides of each sheet. I turn to the first sheet and read...

Dear Janie,
Your intuition is sharp. You have sensed all along that I have not been completely honest with you. It is time now for me to tell you the truth.

At last, I think to myself, before continuing.

I let you believe that Dorothy and I were good friends and I suppose we were at first. I was a skilful pilot, prepared to risk my life for my country, but in many ways I was naive. I had grown up surrounded by family who encouraged me to trust. What I hadn't realised is that people have to earn that trust. You are young and yet I have the sense you have already learned that people are not always what they appear to be. You question everything; I can see it on your face, even when you are silent. It is one of the qualities that convinced me to ask for your help.

I will share my story with you now and leave it to you to make of it what you will. I hope that you will still want to pursue this case for me, despite the clandestine way I have approached our dealings until now. My experience working with the SOE has made me cautious. It's not something you can shake off, that thought that careless words can cost lives.

I know you will have more questions for me once you have read through the rest of this letter and I assure you that this time I will be happy to answer them.

I turn to the next page and let Hugh's words take me back to 1944...

Chapter 20

1944

The sirens seem louder this time. The noise pierces the air, blocking out all the incidental sounds of life. Traffic stops, conversations end. People start running, but their footsteps are silent.

It had been a week of bombing. The targets appeared random, the casualties too many. The word was that the bombs were being dropped merely to save the pilots having to carry them back across the Channel. It was as though the Germans had over-shopped and now it was time to discard the surplus.

They haven't had a chance to meet at all this week. He had several sorties and when he wasn't flying, he was on call on the base. Dancing had to be forgotten for now. But he missed seeing her and she'd written a note.

Can you get away, for an hour? If you can, then meet me at the junction of Watermill Lane and Cross Street at 3pm. I'll wait for you.

Nothing much had happened all morning. He'd walked Scottie around the airfield so many times. Now, if he jangled the lead he was certain the terrier wouldn't even lift his head. He played cards for a while, just for matchsticks. He lost badly, luck wasn't on his side today. He read the note again. Just an hour, it should be possible. He'd tell Christopher of his plan, he could be trusted to keep a secret and at least someone would know where he was, just in case.

By the time he reached Watermill Lane it was a little after 3.15. She'd waited, as she said she would. They embraced, he complimented her on her dress. The bright red polka dot material matched her rosy complexion. On their walks, even their time together in the little fishing boat, she wore trousers. He was proud of her, a woman doing a man's work. But now she looked so feminine, the dress hugging her figure, nipped in tightly around her waist. She clutched a white cardigan around her shoulders. She was in a gay mood, laughing and teasing him.

'You've come without Scottie. It was him I really wanted to see, not you.' Then she kissed him. They walked for a while along Cross Street. She told him how busy she had been with the planting. Some of the early crops were ready to pick, everything was vibrant, it was her favourite time of the year. Neither of them mentioned the week of bombing. That was the darkness and, for now at least, they wanted to stay in the light.

As they turned the corner into East Street the sirens sounded.

'No, not again,' he said, grabbing her arm. People were running in all directions; the air raid warden was ushering them into the shelter. They followed a group, grateful that soon they would be somewhere quieter, safer.

The shelter was in the basement of one of the village school buildings, and once inside, people relaxed a little. They would have to deal with devastation soon enough, but for now they could chat, make a joke. Around the walls were several wooden benches, all taken up by the first arrivals in the shelter. Several of the men had taken their coats off and laid them on the dusty ground so that the women could sit. He didn't have a coat, just his uniform. He worried that her pretty polka-dot dress would be spoilt.

Another woman beckoned to her and edged over, leaving space on her coat so that there was room for two to sit. She nodded in gratitude. Her hand touched the lining of the coat, it felt elegant, expensive. She could only dream of such a coat. She wondered who it belonged to. The woman sitting next to her didn't look wealthy, but then you could never be sure. These were strange times.

The ground shook a little. The bomb had been dropped. The chatter ceased. Some people bent their heads as though in silent prayer. Others looked startled, wide-eyed, fearful. He reached his hand out to hold hers, squeezing her delicate fingers, trying to transmit confidence. They were alive, all would be well.

After a while the air raid warden indicated it was safe for them to leave the shelter. He helped her up, she picked up the coat and wrapped it around her. Although the shelter was dimly lit, he could tell that the coat was a shade of rose. The fabric was soft, maybe even cashmere.

'What are you doing?' he said to her. 'The coat's not yours.'

'I wanted to know the feel of it around me. What do you think?' she did a twirl around. He blushed, he was embarrassed by her behaviour. She was modelling a coat when outside people may have lost everything, their homes, even their lives.

'Don't look so glum,' she said. 'Here, take it.' She removed the coat and thrust it at him. At that moment another woman approached him.

'I think that's mine,' she said, looking expectantly at him.

'Sorry, yes, of course,' he said, brushing the dust from the coat before handing it to her. She smiled in gratitude and nodded.

'Alright for some,' Dorothy said, while the other woman was still in earshot.

Once again, he was embarrassed.

'I need to get back to the base,' he said, a brusqueness had entered his voice.

'What's the rush?' Dorothy said, linking her arm in his. 'At least you could buy me a drink. A little nip of something, after the scare we've had?'

As they filed out of the shelter he saw the woman with the rose-coloured coat ahead of them. She walked slowly, checking from side to side at the buildings that were now nothing but rubble and debris.

'I need to get back to the base,' he repeated. 'I'll see you back to the farm first though, to make sure you're safe?'

'Don't bother,' Dorothy said, an edge to her voice. 'I intend to have some fun first. I'm sure I can find someone to buy me a drink once the pubs open, if you're too miserly.' She let go of his arm and turned to face him. 'Be seeing you,' she said, and winked.

Back at the base he hadn't been missed. He picked Scottie up out of his basket and held him. The terrier wriggled, wanting to be free of his doting master. But Hugh needed to hold on to something to ground his emotions. He was angry with Dorothy, angry with himself. He'd been duped. She wasn't who he thought she was, perhaps he had imposed an ideal on her that was all in his imagination. Then there was the woman in the rose-coloured coat. Their eyes had met for a moment and yet he felt a connection.

Chapter 21

I drop the van off and head straight round to Hugh's lodgings. Rosetta shows me through to the sitting room, where Hugh is dozing in the fireside armchair. She moves quietly, putting her finger to her lips and then, with hand actions, enquires whether I want a drink. I shake my head and she leaves the room. I sit on the sofa, as noiselessly as possible, remove Hugh's letter from my bag and read through it once more. As I reach the last page, I sense a movement beside me and glance up to see that Hugh has woken. He gazes across at me and smiles.

'I didn't mean to wake you,' I say.

'I'm sleeping too much nowadays.'

'Can I get you anything? A drink maybe?'

'No, nothing, thank you. You've read it?' he nods at the letter.

'Yes, several times. What happened to Dorothy?'

'I never saw her again, after that afternoon in the air raid shelter.' He pauses.

'But the SOE flight into France? The Joe who turned up. You saw her then?'

'That Joe wasn't Dorothy. Much of what I told you about that time was true. I met Dorothy. I think I was in love with her for a short while. She was vivacious, impetuous, fun to be with; a spark of light in a time of darkness. She was a land girl, that part is true, but she never worked for the SOE, at least not that I know of.'

'You did though, didn't you?'

'Yes, I flew some of the operatives into France, like I told you. The bombing raid happened, just like I said. But then, I didn't hear from her. I was worried about her, so I visited the farm where she worked. They said she'd up and left. Hadn't told anyone where she was going. I waited for a letter. I was sure she'd get in touch, but when she didn't write, well, life is too short. I got chatting to Winifred at one of the village dances, I recognised her from that night of the bombing raid. We started seeing each other and I fell for her. I realised then that what I'd felt for Dorothy wasn't true love.'

'Winifred? She was the owner of the rose-coloured coat?'

He is gazing across the room now, unaware of his surroundings, as though he is reliving each precious moment of that early passion.

'A few months after Winifred and I met I had to prepare to fly a Joe over to France.'

'Yes, you told me about that.'

'Well, it was Winifred who turned up that night.'

'You let me believe it was Dorothy.'

'I think you chose to believe that. I never said as much. It was a dark day for me. I had to leave the woman I loved in enemy territory and fly back to base, not knowing her fate. It nearly killed me, if I'm honest. It made me realise the strength of my feelings for Winnie and I promised myself there and then that if I ever saw her again I'd ask her to marry me.'

'She returned safely from her mission?'

'I didn't hear from her for several months, I'd given her up for dead, but I thought about her every day. Then one day, there she was. Once she was back from France she came to the base to see me, to let me know she was safe. I knew enough about the importance of secrecy not to ask her where she'd been, or if her mission was successful.'

'Did you ever speak about that time, later, once the war was over?'

'In all our years of marriage we never once spoke about it.'

168

'When did you marry?'

'Straight after the war ended.'

'Did you have any children?'

'No, it was a dreadful sadness for Winnie, but it wasn't to be.'

'So now, after all these years, did you decide that you cared for Dorothy after all? Is that the real reason you're here in Tamarisk Bay? To rekindle a lost love?'

'Far from it. Dorothy took something that wasn't hers.' His face darkens and his fists clench.

'Don't upset yourself, Hugh, remember you need to stay calm. Rosetta will never forgive me if her favourite lodger has to return to hospital.'

'That afternoon, in the air raid shelter. Dorothy stole something precious.'

'Not the coat? You said she handed the coat back.'

'Not the coat, no. But when she tried the coat on and twirled around in it, she must have put her hand in one of the pockets.'

'What did she find? A purse? A wallet?'

'A brooch.'

'She stole a brooch? What makes you so sure?'

'Winifred told me about a brooch she had been given by her grandmother. It was a family heirloom. She said how sad she was that she'd lost it. She felt she'd let her grandmother down. But I didn't know then how or when she had lost it.'

'And now you think Dorothy took it, that day of the air raid? But it could have been anyone in the air raid shelter. You said people put coats on the floor. It could have fallen out, or someone else could have taken it.'

'Do you have the press cutting?'

'Pardon?'

'The press cutting from the left luggage depot?'

I take my notebook from my duffel bag and remove the photocopy of the article. 'I've copied it, I thought it best to keep the original safe in my bedroom drawer at home.'

He smooths the sheet of paper out and points to one of the women in the crowd. 'Dorothy,' he says.

'Yes, Freda Latimer pointed her out. That's Freda there, right next to Dorothy.'

'Do you see what she is wearing?'

'Dorothy?'

'Yes.' Her coat looks shabby, although she is partly hidden by the rest of the group standing in front of her.

'Look closely. What is on the collar?'

'A brooch. Yes, I can see it quite plainly now you point it out.'

'Winifred's brooch. That's how I know that Dorothy stole it. The shape is so distinctive, it's unmistakeable. It was Victorian, very rare and very valuable.'

He is quiet, his eyes fixed on the photo.

'The day of the air raid Winifred must have put it in her coat pocket. She said she lost it when she was on the way to the bank to put it in a safety deposit box. With all the bombings we were experiencing, she was afraid to leave it in her house. Homes were being flattened every week, people's possessions destroyed.'

'But wouldn't she have had it in her handbag, wouldn't that have been safer than putting it in a pocket?'

'A handbag could be easily stolen, during air raids there was a fair amount of pilfering. She would have believed that having it in her pocket was the safest place.'

'But this press cutting is more than twenty years old. If you have known about it all this time, why wait so long? Surely, once you realised you could have gone to the police.'

'No, that's just it. I didn't know. I didn't see this press cutting until my Winnie died. I was going through her papers. She kept diaries, one for every year we were together. I read a few, it was like listening to her voice again. Bittersweet.'

He pauses and I can see he is struggling with his memories.

'Let's take a break, Hugh, I'm worried that all this talking will start your coughing off again. Shall I ask Rosetta to make us a drink?'

'I'm alright. I need to carry on, now that I have started.'

'Well, take it slowly. I'm not in a rush; besides, I don't do shorthand, you know,' I say and smile.

'The cutting fell out of Winnie's diary for 1946. She had known all that time and yet she never told me.'

'Do you know why she kept quiet about it?'

'Winnie was so gentle. Yes, she was courageous, prepared to risk her life for her country, but she was the kindest person I know. She knew it would hurt me to learn that Dorothy had stolen the brooch. I had trusted Dorothy, I thought we were friends.'

'So now what? Do you think Dorothy still has the brooch? Is that what you're hoping?'

'No, I'm certain she won't still have it. Once she found out what it was worth, she would have sold it. That kind of money would have changed her life.'

Some of the pieces of the jigsaw now neatly fit into place. Dorothy must have sold the brooch, transforming not just her life, but that of her brother too. No wonder Kenneth is so keen to keep Hugh and me at arm's length.

It is also possible that Freda's run in with Dorothy could have had something to do with the sudden change of fortune for the Elm family. Libby's contact had also said something about 'rumours'. When a family goes from poverty to affluence overnight there is always a chance that people expect ill-gotten gains to be at the heart of it.

'Why did you say that Dorothy could be in danger?'

'I thought it would help to energise your search for her,' he says and smiles.

'Mm, I'm not sure how I feel about that, but what's done is done. At least I know the truth now. I do know the truth now, don't I, Hugh?'

He nods. 'I'm tired now, Janie. Do you mind if we end our conversation and perhaps you could visit again tomorrow?'

'Before I go, can you just tell me what the point of this search is? If you know that Dorothy took the brooch and you are certain she won't have it anymore, why track her down?'

'Retribution.'

'That's a strong word. What kind of retribution?'

'A punishment that fits the crime,' he says and closes his eyes, which is my cue to leave.

Having no knowledge of criminal law or police procedure is the reason I should take the advice of friends and family and stick with the day job. It appears that a crime has been committed, but there is little proof, barring a blurry photograph in a newspaper article, dated over twenty years ago. What's more, there is a strong likelihood that the item in question has been sold and could be in anyone's hands now, in this country, or even abroad. If I visit DS Bright to ask his opinion I risk opening up lines of enquiry that could lead to more than one person getting into trouble, including me.

If I had a greater understanding of Hugh's motivation it would help. Confronting Dorothy, telling her that Winifred knew the culprit all along; perhaps that's enough.

Hugh's wife showed great generosity of spirit and love for her husband by taking the secret to her grave, or at least that must have been her plan.

Hugh has spoken of 'retribution', punishment for the crime. I'm wondering if it's all too late for that.

Chapter 22

At the denouement of several of Agatha Christie's books Poirot gathers all possible suspects together. He runs through the evidence in front of them and eventually reveals the culprit. Well, in this case, Hugh has told me who the culprit is. What I don't know yet is where she is. It's time to run through the possibilities with Libby and hope that between us we can find a solution.

We meet in *Jefferson's* and as soon as we have drinks in front of us I present her with the facts as I understand them.

'You've been busy,' she says, having listened attentively, nodding her head at regular intervals. 'So, let me get this straight. The real reason Hugh wants to find Dorothy is because she stole a valuable brooch from the woman who Hugh eventually married.'

'That's about the size of it.'

'But Hugh guesses that Dorothy would have sold the brooch by now and spent the proceeds. And that would fit with the various rumours that were kicking about and maybe the reason why Freda got herself slapped. Perhaps she had her suspicions and accused Dorothy to her face?'

'Yes, that's a definite possibility.'

'I still don't get why Hugh is bothered, after all these years.'

'Well, I suppose he feels he owes it to his wife. She protected his feelings for all that time.'

'Mm,' Libby says, using the straw to stir her milkshake, concentration on her face.

'I'm thinking that if there's any way we can get Hugh, Dorothy and Kenneth into a room together, we could force a confession from the Elms,' I say. 'It would also mean we would be on hand to make sure Hugh doesn't get distressed.'

'You're right there, I don't fancy seeing him carted off in an ambulance at this stage of the game.'

'It's not a game, Libby,' attempting a stern voice and failing miserably.

'Sorry, just a figure of speech. Anyway, this is all fanciful. Kenneth is hardly going to agree to it and he's the only one who can tell us where his sister lives.'

'All we can do is revert to my original idea. Stake out Kenneth, follow him and hopefully find this blessed woman. Then we can all relax and return to normality.'

'Is that a touch of impatience I hear in your voice, Mrs Amateur Sleuth? Didn't your dad warn you that being a detective is all about legwork? Look at it this way, you might finally get to use your camera,' she says, winking.

Libby's Mini has seen better days. The rust at the bottom of the doors means the heater has to work overtime to warm the freezing air that blasts in around our feet. Before heading off, I tell Greg our plan.

'You're going to do a stake-out? Crikey, questions like "*How was your day today, darling?*" will never be the same again,' he says, his face breaking into a grin. 'Seriously though, you will be...'

'Careful, yes. And Libby will be there to keep an eye on me.'

'I'm not sure if that makes me feel better or worse.'

'Off you go and concentrate on Brighton winning. Really, we will be fine.'

Having checked the surgery times we know that Kenneth should emerge from the vets shortly after 2pm, but beyond that it's a case of wait and see.

'Does your car have fourth gear?' I say, hoping she'll get the point I'm trying to make.

'Very funny. I don't like driving fast. Anyway, there's no rush. All we're going to do is drive to the vets and sit outside for who knows how long. Did you bring any sweets?'

'Humbugs,' I say, grinning.

'Same to you,' she says, with her hands clenched around the steering wheel and her focus on the road ahead. Her meandering pace is at odds with her usual mile-a-minute demeanour. Seeing her behind the wheel it's as though she has taken on a new persona. No longer is she Libby, the go-getter, the lively chick aiming to make her mark in the male-dominated world of journalism. Instead, this Libby is cautious, timid, as she negotiates her way past buses and vans, her hands gripping the wheel in a classic ten to two position.

'Do you mind me asking why you bought a car if you hate driving so much?'

'A reporter needs a car. I never know where I might need to be to catch the next big story.'

'Mm, we are talking Tamarisk Bay and Tidehaven remember, not a huge metropolis.'

Before she can respond, I spot a Morris Clubman, parked in front of the surgery. 'Look, I'm certain that's his car. Pull over here.'

Libby parks about fifty yards back from the surgery entrance, where we have a clear view of the front door to the vets.

'Humbug?' I say, offering her the bag of sweets.

'Perfect, thanks,' she says, taking one. She unwraps it and throws the wrapper on the floor by her feet.

'What are you doing? No wonder your desk is such a tip. Ever heard of the phrase 'litter lout'?'

'This is my own personal space. If I choose to pollute it, that is my choice,' she says, sucking on her sweet and looking pleased with herself.

'Your poor mum. I can just imagine what your bedroom is like.'

'Mum is delighted to have her only daughter back in the nest. Plus, she never enters the inner sanctum.'

'Afraid she'll catch something?'

'Cheeky,' she says, grinning.

A movement ahead catches my eye. I glance up to see Kenneth leaving the vets and getting into his car.

'Game on,' Libby says, starting the car and gradually easing forward as Kenneth pulls away.

'Good job we're not planning a car chase,' I say, as we slowly make our way down the hill from the surgery in the direction of the seafront. 'And good job most people are at home in front of the telly and not on the road.'

'Stop moaning, he's only three cars in front of us.'

We continue along the seafront in the direction of Tidehaven.

'If we've struck lucky first time, then I retract all my moaning,' I say.

'Don't count your chickens. Maybe he's heading into town to do a spot of shopping?'

As Libby stops speaking the Morris Clubman slows down, indicates left and pulls up in front of a newspaper shop.

'Pull over, quickly, look he's getting out.'

We watch as Kenneth gets out of the car and goes into the shop. Moments later he emerges with a bag in his hand, gets back into his car and prepares to pull away.

'Do you want a bet?' Libby says. 'Are we on a wild goose chase, or not? Winner buys the next lot of milkshakes.'

Five minutes later we are following Kenneth up Ludlow Road, which runs inland from the seafront up towards the top of the town. The roads in this part of Tidehaven are steep and most of the houses are several storeys high, with deep stone steps leading up to them. Kenneth parks in front of a red brick, Victorian terraced house. The paintwork on the front door and windows is chipped and yellowed and there is nothing cheery about the drab plant pots that sit either side of the front door.

'Well, if this is Dorothy's place, then she is certainly no gardener,' Libby says. We are parked opposite the house, maybe at a slight risk of being seen by Kenneth, should he decide to turn in our direction. We watch in silence as Kenneth mounts the steps and knocks on the front door. I realise how apprehensive I must be when my hiccups suddenly decide to kick in.

'Ssh,' Libby says, while I try to control my breath.

'He's not going to hear my hiccups from the other side of the road, is he?' I whisper.

'Why are you whispering then?'

Seconds later the front door opens and a young man appears. He shakes Kenneth's hand and the two of them go inside, closing the door behind him.

'Oh, jeepers,' Libby says, 'milkshakes on you, I think.'

'Hang on a minute, I didn't take you up on the bet.'

'It's not a complete waste of an afternoon though.'

'What do you mean?'

'Well, wasn't he the same dishy bloke who served us in *Jefferson's* the other day?'

'Do you think?'

'I never forget a potential heart-throb,' she says, winking at me. 'At least now I know where he lives, maybe I'll turn up one day, pretending I'm a door-to-door sales lady selling encyclopaedias.'

'I think you're forgetting the reason we're here. We're looking for Dorothy, remember?'

'Sorry, but you can't blame me for getting side-tracked.'

'It's okay, it would have been too much luck to find Dorothy on our first stake-out. Bean, you will have to manage with the budget quality pram, after all,' I say, rubbing my hand on my midriff. 'I think I'll give Hugh his money back and tell him we're off the case.'

We sit for a while in silence, apart from the sound of us munching humbugs.

'Home?' Libby says.

'Or maybe *Jefferson's* to drown our sorrows? Greg won't be back until 6pm at the earliest.'

As Libby prepares to drive away, the door to the property opens again and three people emerge; Kenneth, the young man who had answered the door, and an older woman. I duck down as much as I can inside the car and whisper to Libby, 'Turn away, pretend you haven't seen them.'

The three people get into the Morris Clubman and drive away.

'Crikey,' I say, momentarily lost for words. 'We've found her, Libby, finally we've found her.'

'Are you sure?'

'One hundred percent. I'm certain that was Dorothy Elm.'

Libby turns the engine off as I get my notebook and camera out of my duffel bag.

'You're not going to believe it, but I've missed my chance to get a photo, again,' I say, stuffing the camera back inside the bag. 'At least let me make some notes.'

I turn to the *Where?* section of my notebook and write: *73 Faversham Road.* Then, under the *Who?* section I add: *A man, in his twenties? Clean shaven, long dark hair, no glasses, tall, about six feet? Helps out in Jefferson's?*

'Now what?' Libby says, watching me scribbling.

'No idea. Maybe a drink and a debrief?'

We drive back to Tamarisk Bay and park up near to *Jefferson's*.

'Watch out,' Richie says, as we order our milkshakes. 'This could become an addiction.'

'Better than a few other addictive substances I can think of though,' I say, rummaging around in my bag for my purse. 'Richie, have you got a minute?'

'Sure, good to have an excuse to sit down. How are you doing? How's that bump of yours?'

'Growing,' I say and smile.

'Busy day?' Libby says, raising her voice a little as *Pinball Wizard* blasts out from the jukebox.

'Busy enough,' Richie says, using a cloth to wipe over the table. 'Always good to see my favourite regulars though.'

'You usually have help on a Saturday, don't you?'

'Couldn't manage without some days.'

'The chap who helped out a couple of Saturdays ago, have you taken him on, or was that a one-off?'

'Ray? Yeah, he was in this morning. I can't always afford to pay him for the whole day, plus he said he had something on, some appointment or other, so he disappeared straight after lunch. Why?'

His gaze goes from me to Libby and then he nods his head, 'Ah, I get it, I can see where this is going now. I have no idea if he's already taken, we don't get around to talking about our love lives. But he'll probably be here next

Saturday and don't worry, I won't say a word to him. Your secret is safe with me,' he says grinning.

The café door opens and a foursome come in.

'Sorry, that's my cue to leave,' Richie says.

'Okay, let's concentrate on serious matters,' I say, watching Libby's head swaying in time to the music.

'There's nothing more serious than potential boyfriend material.'

'Just humour me. Do you think we can persuade Hugh to come with us to Faversham Road?'

'I don't think he'll take much persuasion. Once he knows Dorothy's address I can see us being surplus to requirements.'

'How about we don't tell him? Let's think of an excuse to take him out for a drive, arrive at her house and keep everything crossed she's at home.'

'And that she'll let us in.'

'Ah, yes, that too.'

'And my ideal date?' Libby says, her face softening into a dreamy expression.

'He's probably an incidental visitor.'

'Well, he can incidentally visit me any time he likes,' Libby says, grinning.

Greg is euphoric when he bounces in just before 6pm. I've been home a while and preparations for tea are well underway.

'Three nil, three nil,' he chants, taking me in his arms and dancing me around the kitchen.

'Superb,' I say, hoping he won't want to share too much of the detail with me. 'Anything that makes you so happy gets a gold star from me. I'd only planned macaroni cheese, not much of a celebratory supper.'

'Macaroni cheese, my beautiful wife by my side, and a good night on the telly, what else can a man ask for?'

'A beer, maybe?'

'Excellent plan,' he says, going to the fridge. 'What happened with the stake-out? Did it pay off?'

'Er, yes,' I reply, busying myself with laying the table. 'We think we may have found Dorothy's house.'

'Only think?'

'Well, we're fairly certain.'

'So, what's your plan?'

'If we can, I want to try to get Hugh round there. He's the only one who will know for sure.'

'How about tomorrow?' he says, kicking off his boots.

'Well yes, that would be brilliant, why, what are you doing tomorrow?'

'Alex has offered to come round and take a look at the dripping bathroom tap. It's probably a washer or something, but we might have to turn the water off. I was going to suggest you go round your dad's. But maybe you can persuade your client to go on a nice Sunday drive?'

All I need to hope for now is that Libby is happy to give up her Sunday and that between us we can get Hugh and Dorothy together without the sky falling in.

Chapter 23

Rosetta Summer is not convinced that a cold December day is suitable for a '*nice Sunday drive*'. It is possible Hugh has seen through my ruse, and if he has then he is hiding it well. Rosetta fusses around him, suggesting he wears his warmest overcoat, a thick scarf around his neck and his Trilby perched on his head.

'We'll be in the car most of the time, and the heater is pretty efficient,' I say to reassure them both. It was an easy decision to make. We would have struggled to get Hugh's broad frame into the back seat of Libby's Mini, and Bean certainly prevents me from squeezing in anywhere. Libby was also happy to admit that the combination of a sub-zero draught blasting in through her car doors, and a frail chap with a serious chest complaint, could only spell disaster.

'Anyway, Greg doesn't need our car today,' I explained. 'Why do you think he loves our house so much?'

'Because the pub is four minutes' walk away?'

'Exactly.'

We bundle Hugh into the car and head down towards the seafront. One of the many wonderful things about living in a seaside resort is being able to enjoy it in the winter. On summer days we hide away, while the town is flooded with day-trippers from London. They queue outside the many fish and chip shops, lose their pennies and pounds playing the amusements on the Pier, and brave the shingle beach, regardless of the weather. But when winter arrives, the town belongs to the locals again. Today the whole length of the seafront is peopled with dog-walkers, elderly folk enjoying their Sunday afternoon constitutional, and families blowing away the cobwebs.

'You're taking me to see Dorothy, aren't you?' Hugh says, bringing my mind back to my companions. His question distracts me momentarily and I have to brake abruptly when a young boy steps off the pavement suddenly, just as my car is passing him. His father pulls him back, tugging at his arm, shouting at him. I don't hear the words, but the father's angry face and the boy's instant tears tell me all I need to know.

'Sorry everyone,' I say, as we gently move forward again.

'Should you be driving?' Hugh says, turning towards me. He is in the front passenger seat, with Libby sitting directly behind him.

'The boy took me by surprise,' I say, my face flushing.

'I'm not suggesting you are a bad driver,' Hugh continues, reading my mind. 'It's just, well, your baby...' He pauses, perhaps struggling for the most appropriate phrase.

'You're right, it won't be long before the space between Bean and the steering wheel will be non-existent.'

'What about the van?' Libby pipes up from the back seat. 'Will you have to stop working at the library?'

'Not sure, maybe. Although I have a cunning plan involving your grandmother,' I say, catching Libby's eye in the rear-view mirror.

'You didn't answer my question about Dorothy,' Hugh says, an irritation in his voice I haven't heard before.

I'm tempted not to respond as we are almost at our destination. 'We're not certain of anything right now, Hugh. It's possible the house we're planning to visit is where Dorothy lives. If we're right, there's a slim chance she'll be home and an even slimmer chance she'll open the door to us.'

He doesn't reply, instead he starts to cough. The coughing is raucous and persistent. He struggles to catch his breath and when he does breathe there is a loud rasping wheeze from his chest. As soon as I see a space on the roadside, I pull over. Libby immediately jumps out of the car, opens Hugh's passenger door and crouches down to his level. We look at Hugh's contorted face and exchange a glance with each other, sharing mutual concern and fear. An image flashes through my mind of me sitting in the police interview room, trying to explain to DS Bright why I was driving a poorly man around the streets of Tidehaven on a bitterly cold Sunday afternoon, and what I said or did that caused him to stop breathing and die.

But thankfully, it looks as though it won't come to that, at least not on this occasion, as gradually the coughing settles down and then stops completely.

'We'd better take you home,' I say, looking at Libby, who nods in agreement.

'No,' Hugh says, firmly, 'I'll be fine, really. But could you switch the car heater off?'

Hugh was right. I'd been so intent on keeping him warm I hadn't realised how stuffy the car had become. It was only when Libby opened the door and the cold, fresh air flooded in, that Hugh was able to get control of his breathing.

'Well, if we do get to meet Dorothy, we'll have to hope she doesn't live in a hot house,' I say lightly, trying to defuse the tension.

Five minutes later we are parked opposite 73 Faversham Road.

'Is that the house?' Hugh asks. 'I've waited a long time for this day.' His voice is heavy with emotion. It's as though he is about to be reunited with a lost love and yet everything he's told me about Dorothy suggests anger and regret are more appropriate emotions.

'You two wait here, or better still I'll find my own way home. I can get a taxi,' he says, turning to open the car door.

'Oh no, you don't,' I say. 'We haven't come this far together to leave you now. We'll go together or not at all.'

He grunts and shuffles in his seat. 'I need to do this on my own. The conversation I plan to have with Dorothy is private. I wanted you to find her for me and you have. I'm grateful for that and I'll pay you, as promised. But I'm asking you to go now. To be brutally honest, what Dorothy and I have to discuss is none of your business.'

'Sorry, Hugh,' I say, 'but you've made it my business.'

I turn to Libby and indicate to her to get out of the car. We walk around to Hugh's side of the car and I open the passenger door.

'Will you be joining us?' I say, pleased to be sounding in control of a situation that could easily spin off in an unpleasant direction at any point.

Hugh looks up at us, clearly disgruntled. After a few moments where we are all silent, he says, 'you haven't given me much choice. Let's get this over with.' He stretches his legs out of the car and stands.

'Are you feeling okay?' I ask him, aware that he is looking pale.

He shakes his head, but doesn't reply.

Taking the lead, I cross the road, Hugh follows me and Libby brings up the rear. Now that I am close to the house, the poor state of repair is even more obvious. The plant pots that stand either side of the front door are chipped and covered with mildew. A few brown leaves sit on top of the soil in one of the pots and the other is empty, apart from a few broken twigs. The paint on the door must once have been white, but now it is various shades of murky cream and dull yellow. The sea salt that blasts through from the seafront throughout the winter means that properties need repainting often, but this house isn't only suffering from the salt air. There is no door knocker, just a round buzzer, with a sign below it that reads, *Press me.* I glance at Libby before pressing it, her face reflecting the apprehension I am also feeling. There is no obvious noise from the buzzer, so I press it again. It is possible that the bell is ringing deep within the house somewhere, in which case my double pressing won't get us off to a good start with Dorothy.

After a few moments, during which I am holding my breath, I can hear footsteps. There is the noise of a chain being slid across and then the door opens a little, enough for a conversation, but not enough to allow me to see the person on the other side of the door.

'Yes, who is it?' a woman's voice says.

'Excuse us, but we are looking for Dorothy Elm,' I say.

'Wrong house,' she says and swiftly closes the door again.

'Great,' Libby says. 'Now what.'

Until this moment, Hugh has been standing below me on the second step of the small stone staircase leading up to the front door. Now, he moves forward, putting his hand on my shoulder, indicating to me to stand aside. I step backwards, leaving the top step free for him and watch as he presses the buzzer again, firmly.

Once more we hear the chain slide across and the door eases open a crack.

'If you don't leave, I'll call the police,' the woman says.

'That's fine with me, Dorothy,' Hugh says. 'You go right ahead. We have plenty to tell them, don't we?'

There is silence, both from inside the house and from the three people standing outside. For a few moments it's as though the whole world has frozen, as no cars pass by and the only sound is the call of a distant seagull. Then there is the sound of the chain again, and the door opens fully to reveal a woman about fifty years old, dressed in a patterned housecoat, tied tightly around her narrow waist. Over the top of the housecoat she is wearing a thick cardigan that has one or two holes near the neck, where a moth or two has had a feast. One of the sleeves of the cardigan is bulging with the edge of a handkerchief showing below the cuff. Her face is heavily lined, her thin mouth closed, a sour expression in her eyes.

'Hugh,' she says, a brittle emphasis on the single word.

'Yes,' he says, his voice thick with emotion.

'I'm Janie Juke and this is Libby Frobisher. We're friends of Hugh,' I say, offering my hand out to shake hers.

She stands with both hands in the pockets of her housecoat, leaving the three of us squashed into the area just inside the front door.

'We're sorry to intrude, it being a Sunday and everything, but can we come in?' Libby says.

'Friends, eh?' Dorothy says, sizing up Libby and me as if we were auditioning for a part in a play. 'Thought you'd need back up, did you, Hugh?'

Hugh appears to have lost the ability to speak or move.

'Mrs Elm, it might be easier if we weren't having this conversation in your hallway?' I say, putting my hand on Hugh's back to try to gently ease him forward.

'Who said we were going to have a conversation?' Dorothy says. 'And it's not Mrs Elm. Elm was my maiden name.'

'You've married?' Hugh says, finally appearing to have found his voice.

Dorothy doesn't respond, but turns away from us and starts to walk along the hallway to the back of the house. 'Now you're here, you might as well come in,' she says.

We follow her down the dark hallway and in through a doorway, which leads to a dining room. In the centre of the room is a large oval mahogany table, with six chairs positioned around its edges. The chairs are different shapes and sizes, none matching. Across the centre of the table is a narrow piece of lace and on the centre of the lace sits a glass fruit bowl, containing a single shrivelled apple.

Dorothy pulls out one of the chairs and sits down. Taking her lead Libby and I also sit opposite her, leaving only Hugh still standing.

'I would have preferred to come alone,' Hugh says.

'Couldn't get rid of your young hangers-on, eh?' Dorothy says, a sneer on her face.

'Mrs Juke and her friend have been very kind to me,' Hugh says.

'I bet they have,' the sarcasm in Dorothy's voice is undisguised.

'You two must have a lot to discuss, why don't Libby and I make us all a drink? Would you mind us rummaging around in your kitchen, Mrs...?' I say, not knowing what to call her and certain that using a Christian name at this stage would not be well received.

'You can call me Dorothy. There's no milk, but if you don't mind your tea black, that's fine with me. The kitchen's down the hall, second on the right.'

Dorothy ushers us out, closing the door behind us.

Chapter 24

Libby and I hover in the hallway for a moment, keeping as still as possible, with our faces up against the closed door.

'Can you hear what they're saying?' she whispers.

I shake my head and taking her hand, I lead us both to the kitchen.

The size of Dorothy's kitchen would make any chefs envious. Floor and wall cupboards cover almost all available space, except for a large cooker and an even larger fridge. There is a small window above the sink, with net curtains that have seen better days. With little or no natural light coming in, the room is dim and uninviting. I imagine how different it could be with a bustling cook, beavering away making cakes and biscuits, warming the space and filling the whole house with wafts of cinnamon, vanilla and mixed spice. The thought of it makes my stomach rumble.

'Are we going to make a drink? Or shall we creep back and wait outside the door in case the conversation gets heated?' Libby says.

'See if you can find any coffee,' I say, opening some of the cupboards. 'Pots and pans, plates, glasses, but no food. I thought I was bad at managing a store cupboard, but Dorothy hits a whole other level.'

I open the fridge, which has an unopened jar of mustard, a part used tin of baked beans and a few mouldy carrots.

'She's right about the milk,' Libby says, peering into the fridge as I hold the door open. 'I'll put the kettle on and then I think we should take the opportunity to go exploring.'

'Exploring?'

190

'Yes, we should have a nose in some of the other rooms, while Dorothy and Hugh are occupied, so to speak. You never know what we might find.'

'You're worse than me.'

'I'm a journalist, remember.'

'Mm, okay. But don't touch anything, whatever you do.'

'Did you bring your camera?'

'Oh, crikey, I don't believe it. I've left it in my bag and my bag is in the dining room. Great, another photo opportunity missed.'

'Don't worry, use your powers of observation and memory. You take the room on the left, I'll go right and we'll meet back here in two minutes.'

'Two minutes?'

'Yes, that's how long the kettle will take to boil, by which time Dorothy will be expecting our return. We don't want her to come looking for us, do we?'

The room I go into appears to be a study of sorts. The walls are lined with bookshelves and in the centre of the room is an old-fashioned bureau, made of mahogany or similar, with a green leather blotter on top, providing a writing area. I open a few of the drawers, trying to be as quiet as possible. The drawers are empty, as are the bookshelves. But in one corner of the room is a stack of cardboard boxes, each taped closed with sticky tape and a large wooden tea chest, which appears to be full of documents and magazines.

Assuming my two minutes are up I return to the kitchen to find Libby already there, pouring the hot water into a couple of mugs.

'Anything?' I ask her.

'It's weird. There's a sitting room, but the armchairs and settee are covered in sheets, no pictures on the wall, not even a clock. It doesn't look like anyone plans on relaxing in there today. What about you? Find anything?'

'No, nothing. Her study is empty, bar a load of boxes. Nothing in the desk drawers, no ornaments, or photos.'

'You opened the drawers? I thought you said not to touch?'

'I didn't, I just opened the drawers. Look, let's take the drinks through and see if we can sus out what they've been talking about.'

I follow Libby through to the dining room and as we approach we hear Dorothy's voice, high pitched and piercing. 'No-one will ever believe you,' she shouts.

I don't wait for a reply, but push open the door to find Dorothy standing, her arms raised and a vicious expression on her face. Hugh is seated at the far end of the dining table, glaring at Dorothy as though he has been punched.

'Drinks, anyone?' Libby says, lightly.

They turn to look at us and I hesitate in the doorway, wondering who will make the next move.

'We are leaving,' Hugh says. 'I will be back, Dorothy. You can bank on that.'

'Do what you like, it won't make any difference now,' she says, walking around Libby and holding the door open.

Once the three of us are back in the car, I turn to Hugh and notice his hands are shaking.

'What happened between you two?'

'I don't want to talk about it. Just take me home, please.'

'Home? Back to your lodgings, you mean?'

He nods and turns away from me to gaze out of the window, but I have the feeling he is not seeing anything as we drive back to Tamarisk Bay in silence; our visit resulting in more questions than answers.

We drop Hugh back at his lodgings, with a warning glance for Rosetta. We watch him slowly climbing the stairs to his bedroom, his shoulders slumped forward and his head bent. For a man who is no stranger to great feats of bravery, today he looks as though he has lost not just one battle, but the entire war.

A welcome aroma greets me as I push open our front door.

'How did you know what I'd been dreaming of on the way home?' I say, walking through to the kitchen.

'Telepathy. All good partnerships have it, you know,' Greg says, taking my coat and scarf and gesturing to me to sit. 'One or two?'

'Need you ask? Two, of course.'

He slides a plate over to me with two hot crumpets, the butter still melting in a golden puddle in the centre of each one.

'I knew there was a reason I married you,' I say, planting a sticky kiss on his lips, after taking my first bite.

'How is my super sleuth of a wife? Did the plan work? Have you located the elusive Dorothy?'

'Let me finish these while they're hot and then I will tell you all. How about Alex, do we have non-dripping taps now?'

'Taps all present and correct, madam. We owe him some kind of thank you. I did buy him a pint, but he wouldn't take any money. Maybe we can ask him round for supper one night?'

'Does he have a girlfriend?'

'Not as far as I know. Why, you're not planning to matchmake, are you?'

'I don't think he's Libby's type and anyway, I have a feeling Libby's heart is presently set on someone else entirely, but Becca is due home from uni soon, isn't she?' I say, smiling. 'Tell you what, how about we ask Alex and Becca and your mum and dad at the same time. Then we can talk godparenting and see if your dad is happy to still give you a hand decorating Bean's room. Didn't you say he'd offered?'

'Okay, sounds good. I'll talk to them. Now, come on, tell me what happened with Hugh, don't keep me on tenterhooks. I quite like the idea of my wife as an investigator, it's like having a ready-made television series to catch up with on a nightly basis.'

I push my empty plate aside and get out my notebook.

'Who would have thought it?' he says, interrupting.

'What?'

'Look at you, making lists, following a system.'

'What do you mean? I'm excellent at systems, that's why I'm such a great librarian,' I say, defensively.

'It's a shame you don't apply it to all aspects of our life, like shopping lists,' he says, grinning. He is teasing me about last week when I made a list, but went shopping without it and we had no butter for three days.

'Point taken. So, we were right, it was Dorothy's house and Hugh persuaded her to let us in. Then, while the two of them were talking, well, more arguing than talking, Libby and I went exploring.'

'For exploring I should read being nosey?'

'Needs must. But what do you think of this? Dorothy's place was like no-one lived there. There was no food in the cupboards, no food in the fridge. Both the rooms we looked in had stuff packed away in boxes. Why would someone live like that?'

'They wouldn't.'

'So, what do you think it means?'

'That's the point, isn't it? They wouldn't live like that, unless they are planning not to live there anymore. Unless they are planning to move?'

194

Chapter 25

When the library van door opens the next morning the last person I expect to see entering is Dorothy. She strides in and presents herself at the counter, glaring directly at me. Her camel coloured coat has a grimy mark on the collar and one of the buttons is hanging by a thread. A brown woollen scarf is wrapped around her neck and she is wearing a brown beret, which makes me think of school uniform.

'How did he rope you in then?' she says.

'I'm sorry?'

'Your so-called *friend*, Hugh Furness.'

'Mrs ...' I hesitated.

'I go by the name of Mrs Madden, but like I said yesterday, you can call me Dorothy. I'm not like some, with their airs and graces.'

'Well, Dorothy, I'm not too sure what it is you think you know, but the relationship between Hugh and me is private.'

'I'll bet it is. Your husband knows about him, does he?'

'I don't like the tone of your voice, Dorothy. Perhaps you'd like to take a seat for a moment and we can start again. Maybe we could start with 'Good morning'?'

I pull out the spare chair from behind the counter and offer it to her.

'I'm happy standing. From the looks of that bump of yours it's you who needs to take the weight off. So, come on, tell me. Is he paying you?' Her expression is sneering, her voice acid.

'As I said, the relationship between Hugh and me is private.'

'He's free with his money is our Hugh. You know it's not even his? That wife of his was the one with the rich family. Handy she went and died on him and left him the lot.'

With all the thoughts running around in my mind, the over-riding one is how to get this unpleasant woman to leave.

'How about I tell you a few home truths?' she says. 'The man you're working for is a liar.'

For the second time I'm being told not to trust Hugh.

'I'm pleased you are here, Dorothy,' I say, deciding to compound the lying that appears to surround this case. 'I'd like to ask you a few questions, concerning a brooch.'

She glares at me, before a sickly smirk spreads over her face.

'What brooch would that be?'

'I think you know the answer to that.'

'Why don't you spell it out for me?'

'You stole a brooch. It was when you were a land girl, during the war.'

'Ha,' she pretends to laugh, but the sound is hollow. 'Now let me think, I'm reckoning you weren't even born back then, were you?'

'Hugh has proof. He's shown it to me.'

'Proof, eh? Well, you need to be careful, throwing accusations around. Could get yourself into trouble and I'm sure your dad wouldn't like that now, would he?'

My heart starts to thump uncomfortably fast, as the adrenalin floods through my body.

'How did you find me, Dorothy? Who told you I worked here?'

'Oh, you're not hard to find. You should know all about tracking people down, done a touch of that yourself, haven't you?'

'Kenneth,' I say, sensing some of the pieces of my puzzle slotting into place. Kenneth would have told his sister everything. It would have been no surprise to Dorothy when Libby and I turned up at her house. 'What happened to the brooch, Dorothy?'

'Now, I don't think that's any business of yours, is it?'

'I could make it police business though.'

'So, the young lady is foolish enough to threaten me. Well, think again, you're a little out of your depth here. Let me guess the story that Hugh has cooked up. I expect he's told you that I took something so precious from his wife that she carried the sadness to her death bed.'

I can sense my hiccups coming on and start deep breathing to try to control them. Dorothy gives me a quizzical glance. 'Not going to faint on me, are you?' She sounds genuinely concerned, any bitterness gone from her voice.

I pour myself some water and sit down, while she remains standing.

'Why did you get yourself mixed up with all this?' she says, 'You could walk away now, pretend you've never met either of us.'

I shake my head, wondering what it is she is so desperate to hide. Throughout the time we have been speaking no customers have come into the van. But now the door opens and Ethel Latimer walks in and approaches the counter.

'I won't disturb you, I can see you're busy,' she says quietly, taking a sideways glance at Dorothy.

'Did you need to exchange a book?' I ask her, knowing the answer as there is no book in her hand and no space for one in the small handbag she is carrying.

'I just wanted to let you know about mum,' she says, with an emphasis on the final word.

'I might be a little while here,' I say, aware that Dorothy is watching us.

At that moment Dorothy puts a hand on my arm, 'You carry on and speak to your friend. I only came to tell you one thing,' she says, as I pull my arm away from her.

Before I can respond she walks towards the door.

'Wait, you haven't told me anything,' I say, trying to keep the desperation from my voice.

'Tell Hugh he won't be seeing me again. I'm off and this time he'll never find me,' she says. Then she opens the door and leaves, before I can say another word.

'What was all that about?' Ethel asks me.

'Believe it or not, that was Dorothy Elm, the woman who slapped your mother-in-law round the face, twenty-five years ago.

'Goodness, was it? I wish I'd known that while she was standing right here beside me. I'd have given her a piece of my mind and no mistake.'

I take a few more sips of water, trying to reconcile my emotions, which are a mixture of relief and frustration.

'Are you alright?' she asks, 'you've gone very pale. She's upset you hasn't she? Seems like not much has changed after all these years, she's still got a nasty streak in her.'

I take some gentle breaths and force my face into a smile to reassure her. 'What was it you were going to tell me about Freda?'

'I was wondering whether you had a chance to talk to Phyllis? Remember I told you the two of them have been chatting about the old days.'

'No, events have kind of overtaken me. Mind you, I'm surprised Phyllis made it over to visit, she's done something to her ankle. She was hobbling the last time I saw her. I can't imagine that getting on and off a bus would have been much fun for her.'

'Well, you know Phyllis better than I do, but I'd say there isn't much that will stop her once she's put her mind to something.'

'Has Freda spoken any more to you? About the incident with Dorothy?'

'Bits and pieces come out, now and then. She mixes up the past with the present a lot of the time, so it's difficult to be sure what she's trying to say.'

'Was there something specific?'

Ethel nods. That press cutting you left, the one with the photo of the two of them. Well, she keeps it tucked inside the front of her Bible. She's always kept a Bible beside her bed, not that I've ever seen her reading it. But these last few days she keeps taking the article out and points at the photo, stabbing at it with her finger, saying, *"lies, it was all lies"*.'

An investigator has to focus primarily on the evidence. Supposition and hearsay don't stand up in court and are no basis for a conviction. Later on that day, when the library van is quiet, I take out my notebook and read through the concrete evidence I have gathered.

Of course, for evidence to be relevant, there has to be proof a crime has been committed. I have proof that Dorothy was wearing a brooch that looks as though it could be valuable, but I only have Hugh's accusation the brooch belonged to his wife. Everything else: the suggestion that Dorothy is in danger; Kenneth's strange behaviour; and Freda's memory of her encounter with Dorothy are all circumstantial bits and pieces that don't add up to very much.

There is only one route left open to me now and that is to confront Hugh and give him one final opportunity to tell me the whole truth and nothing but.

Chapter 26

Rosetta Summer answers the door at Hugh's lodgings, welcoming me in with a flamboyant wave of her hand.

'Oh, it is lovely that you come today. Mr Furness is still in his room, but I make coffee and we can all sit together,' she says.

Her greeting is heartfelt, but on this occasion I need to have Hugh to myself, to be able to talk freely.

'Thank you, that sounds very nice. But, could I have a little time with Mr Furness? I have some personal family business to discuss with him.'

'Of course, of course. You come to see him, not me. I understand,' she says, her voice deflated, the brightness faded from her face.

'No, not at all. If Hugh and I could have a few moments to chat, then if you'd like to join us...?' I hesitate, realising I am issuing an invitation to the poor woman in her own home.

While we are hovering in the hallway I hear footsteps and glance up to see Hugh, slowly descending the staircase.

'Janie,' he says, his body language still that of a man who is defeated.

'I thought we could have a quick chat,' I say, 'if you're feeling well enough?'

'Oh, I'm just fine,' he says, his voice belying his words. 'Mrs Summer, would you mind if the two of us used the sitting room for our conversation?'

'I will bring you coffee,' she says, smiling politely and then she turns and walks off to the kitchen.

Hugh and I sit opposite each other, in the velour-covered armchairs that are positioned either side of the fireplace.

'Hugh, I'll come straight to the point. You've told me a lot about your past, but I think there's a lot more you haven't told me.' I look directly at him, watching for his reaction.

He avoids eye contact for a few moments, gazing down at a piece of white fluff on his dark grey trousers and flicking it onto the floor. Then he looks up at me.

'You are astute. Yes, I have misled you.'

'I need much more than that, Hugh, I need to know why you have chosen to mislead me. It's time for you to explain to me all that happened between you and Dorothy back in 1944.'

Before he can answer there is a knock on the door. I get up to open it and in walks Rosetta, carrying a tray with a pot of coffee, cups and saucers and a plate of freshly baked shortbread. She puts the tray down on the sideboard and leaves the room, without saying a word.

'I feel guilty, asking Rosetta to stay out of her own sitting room,' I say.

'I can tell you all about guilt, my dear,' Hugh says, bowing his head, his voice thick with emotion.

'There's more to the story than you've shared with me so far, isn't there?'

'I should have realised when I first met you.'

'What?' I ask him.

'I employed you because of your tenacity. I should have been more open with you from the start and I'm sorry for that. But it will have made little difference to the ending.' There is a desperate sadness, even exhaustion in his voice.

'Nothing has ended yet, Hugh. I promised you I'd find Dorothy. Well, I've done that. But now you need to tell me the real reason you hired me.'

His hands are in his lap and I notice they are shaking.

'About eighteen months after Winnie and I were married I received a letter from Dorothy. She had tracked me down through the RAF. The day the letter arrived was the same day Winnie had her second miscarriage.'

Tears are now running down his face, along the side of his nose, dropping onto his chin. I have to stop myself from jumping up and wiping them away for him.

'I'm so sorry, Hugh. That must have been difficult for you both.'

'More difficult when I read the contents of Dorothy's letter. She told me I had a son.'

I suppress a gasp, not wanting to distract him from sharing his painful memories.

'Dorothy was demanding money. She said that life was very difficult, trying to manage on her own with a baby. She asked me to send money once a month. I didn't show Winnie the letter, I knew it would break her heart to think I had a child out there somewhere. I wrote back to Dorothy, telling her that of course I would send money to help her care for my son, but in return I wanted to know about the child. I asked for a photo, begged her to tell me what he was like. Of course, if I'd been single I would have offered to do the decent thing and marry her, but I told her that wasn't possible. I said if she told me where she was living I would visit. I wanted to see my son.'

'What happened? Did you meet him?'

He shakes his head, using the handkerchief to dry his face. His hands are still trembling and he looks away from me, avoiding my gaze. 'Dorothy wrote back saying she would never let me see him. The letter was ranting, almost hysterical. She said I had betrayed her by marrying someone else. All she wanted was money and if I didn't send it she would tell my wife everything.'

'Oh, Hugh,' I say, searching for the right words and failing miserably. 'So, you've been paying her ever since?'

'I was to send the money to a PO Box at the main Tidehaven post office. I guessed she must have been living somewhere nearby, but I couldn't be certain. Winnie must have known all along. I couldn't understand why she would have been taking the *Tidehaven Observer,* but she must have guessed something. When she died and I found the press cutting, I realised we had both kept secrets from each other. Twenty-five years of secrets and lies.'

His gaze is down and his voice is almost a whisper. I can't bear to see him brought so low.

'She's taken an awful lot of money from you over the years. I guess now you have told her that the payments will stop she has realised she will have to move?'

'What do you mean?'

'When we were there the other day, at her house, Libby and I took a look around. All her stuff is in boxes. Then Dorothy came to see me at the library van. She told me to tell you that you will never see her again. She is moving somewhere you will never find her.'

His expression is pained now, as though he is torturing himself by replaying the memories. 'She has played me like a fool. For twenty-five years I've sent her money, to help support my son. A son I was never allowed to meet, I didn't even know his name. I used to imagine what he looked like, wonder if I'd recognise myself in him. She never told me about his schooldays, his friends, his hopes or his dreams. And do you know why that is?'

When I don't respond he continues, with vitriol in his voice, 'The reason is, my dear, that I don't have a son. How about that? Dorothy has had the last laugh alright. Finally, I am here with a chance to meet him and he doesn't exist.'

His voice has become louder, almost shrill, his breathing quickens and I notice he is sweating. Then his cough starts, the moment I have been fearing all along. As I move over to him to put my hand on his back, to offer some comfort, his cough gets louder. The sitting room door opens and Rosetta rushes in.

'Oh no,' she wails. 'I call an ambulance?' She stands on the other side of Hugh, who is now struggling to breathe in-between the coughing. I nod at her, our eyes meeting above Hugh's head. I listen solemnly to her making the phone call from the hallway, as I continue to rub Hugh's back, talking quietly to him, reminding him to breathe slowly, in the hope that a soothing voice may help to calm him.

After half a lifetime of hoping that one day he would meet his only son, to be told that he never existed, is the cruellest of blows.

Chapter 27

An hour or so later Hugh is being well cared for in hospital, back on oxygen and I am making my way to the *Tidehaven Observer* offices. Fortunately, Libby is at her desk.

'Janie,' she says, her face lighting up and then changing into a frown when she sees the concern on my face.

'Can you get away for a while?' I whisper, having already piqued the attention of her colleague at the neighbouring desk.

She grabs her jacket and handbag and follows me out of the building.

'Where are you parked?' I ask her. 'Did you drive in or catch the bus?'

'I drove, I'm due to go over to Brightport. Some competition to do with cake-making or some such nonsense. What's going on, Janie, you look really frazzled?'

'I'll explain on the way.'

'Where are we headed?'

'73 Faversham Road

'Righto, I'm on it.'

As we drive up to Dorothy's house I fill Libby in on the day's events, as well as the encounter I had with Dorothy yesterday.

'What a cow,' she says.

'Don't hold back,' I say, smirking.

'She's made the poor man believe he has betrayed his wife for years, handed over money, all for nothing. He's held on to his hopes for more than twenty years and now she's told him there is no son. But you think Hugh does have a son, don't you?'

'We've seen him.'

'The dishy bloke?'

'I'm sure of it. Kenneth's job was to keep Hugh from finding out the truth. Plus, I reckon the boy doesn't even know what his mother has been up to for all those years. I'm so mad with myself that I didn't get a photo. If I'd caught the three of them on camera, then Dorothy wouldn't be able to deny it. As it is we're going to struggle to get an admission from her.'

'Will Hugh be okay?'

'He's not a well man and all this turmoil isn't helping.'

We park outside Dorothy's house and I am barely out of the car before Libby is pressing the buzzer.

'I'm a girl on a mission,' she says, turning to me and grinning.

We hear the chain going on, then the door opens a crack.

'Oh, it's you two,' Dorothy says, 'well, there's a surprise.'

'Let us in, Dorothy. We have some information for you that is to your advantage,' I say.

She slides the chain back, opens the door wide and stands back for us to enter.

'What's that then?' she asks.

'I'm not speaking to you standing here on the doormat. How about you do the courteous thing and show us in?' I say.

She makes a grumbling noise, turns and walks along the hallway and we follow. Once inside the dining room, we stand beside the mahogany dining table, where the single apple is still on display, now even more shrivelled.

'Hugh is in hospital,' I say, watching for a reaction.

She raises an eyebrow and then pulls out a chair and sits down. 'Might as well take the weight off.' She gestures to us to sit on the opposite side of the table.

'He's extremely poorly, the doctors are concerned about him,' I continue, ignoring Libby's questioning glance.

'What's it to me?' Dorothy says.

'Do you really want your son to lose the chance to meet his father?' I say.

'What son?' she says.

'Come on, Dorothy, don't play games with us. We know you've lied to Hugh. You do have a son - his son.'

'How dare you call me a liar? You'd better have some proof. I could do you for defamation of character.'

'Dorothy, do you realise there is a strong possibility that Hugh could die?'

'We're all going to die,' she says.

'I don't believe you are a bad person, Dorothy. This is your opportunity to make amends,' I say, trying to keep my voice objective, yet persuasive.

'Why should I want to make amends? My life has been tough. He was alright, with his fancy wife and all her money.'

For a few moments none of us speak. Dorothy glares directly at me, as though she is trying to weigh up her options. I hold her gaze, wondering which of us will be the first to surrender.

'Raymond,' she says, her voice almost reverential. 'He's a good boy.'

I raise an eyebrow.

'Oh, I know, he's a young man now, but he'll always be my boy.' There is a softness in her voice I haven't heard before.

'Hugh doesn't want to take him from you, Dorothy. Is that what you're frightened of? Is that why you lied to him?'

She shrugs her shoulders.

'You know that his wife had two miscarriages, Raymond is Hugh's only child, his only son.'

'She might not have had children, but she had a husband, didn't she? That's more than I had.'

'What about Mr Madden?' Libby pipes up.

'There never was a Mr Madden. When I came back here, pregnant with Raymond, I had to say something. So I told everyone I'd met a pilot, got married, then he died in the war. Proper war hero he was.'

'Is that what Raymond believes? That his dad was a war hero?' Libby asks.

Dorothy nods.

'Well, it's true enough,' I say. 'Hugh was a war hero. Flying dangerous missions, taking risks to save lives.'

'I made the mistake of taking my mother's maiden name,' she says, her voice stern again. 'Then some busybody got suspicious, accused me. I soon put her right.'

Freda Latimer's face comes to my mind, another puzzle piece clicked into place.

'Do you still love your poetry, Dorothy?' I ask her.

Her eyes widen, and I detect a quiver in her voice. 'Poetry? What do I want with poetry?'

'You used to write it, didn't you? Hugh told me how he loved listening to you reading verses out to him.' I pause, watching for her reaction.

'I was a young girl, with fancy ideas. Life knocks the stuffing out of you. You wait and see,' she says, gesturing at my midriff.

'Stopping your son from meeting his father would be the act of a vindictive person. Don't be that person, Dorothy. Find the gentleness that was in your heart all those years ago. It's still there somewhere, isn't it?'

'It's hard being a mother, harder still when you're doing it on your own. If I didn't have Kenneth...' she stops mid-sentence, her gaze drifting away from us, towards the windows. A dark cloud is passing across the house, blocking out the fading light, so that each of us becomes a silhouette against the wintry sky. We have reached an impasse.

'We're going to leave you now, Dorothy. But before we go, I am going to ask you one more time to take this chance to be honest with your son. He will thank you for it in years to come and I think that in your heart you know that.'

She stands and in a business-like fashion walks to the door, opening it and gesturing to us to walk ahead of her.

'Will you give it serious thought? Before it's too late for all of you?' I say, grasping my last opportunity to persuade her.

I don't see her reaction, if indeed there is one, because a few moments later she is showing us out of the front door, without another word.

'How do you think that went?' Libby asks, as we get into her car.

'You were surprisingly quiet.'

'I thought you had control of the situation. You're better at keeping calm, so I decided it was best not to stick my oar in and mess it all up.'

'I didn't feel calm. I felt furious, if I'm honest. Okay, so Hugh has made mistakes, told lies, kept secrets. But when it comes to dishonesty I think Dorothy would win first prize. Poor Raymond.'

It seems my powers of persuasion are more than adequate.

I would love to have been present when Dorothy told her son the truth about his father, to hear her explain how Hugh had supported them for twenty-five years, without once being able to meet his only child. But it is enough for me to know that, finally, father and son will meet. The note that advises me of this happy development is there, on dad's doormat, with the remainder of his post. It's been hand delivered, but offers no clue as to who wrote it, or put it through the letterbox. I have barely two hours' notice to get myself and Libby over to the hospital, so that I can at least be present, albeit briefly, when Hugh meets his son for the first time.

When Libby and I meet Raymond in the foyer of the hospital I am taken by his demeanour, which is polite, almost chivalrous, in stark contrast to his mother. Libby is taken in quite another way. She had spent the previous hour worrying about her make-up, turning the collar of her coat up and then down again.

'You do know why we are meeting Raymond, don't you?' I say.

'Of course I do.'

'Well, I'm guessing his mind will be focused on things other than women.'

'First impressions and all that,' she says, taking a mirror from her handbag and checking her lipstick for the hundredth time.

He arrives promptly, wearing dark green bell-bottomed trousers, cowboy boots and a cream Aran sweater. I have a brief moment of concern he might overheat in the sweater once he is at his father's bedside. On the two previous occasions we have seen him his hair has hung loose, but today he has it tied back in a pony tail, accentuating his strong jawline and dark sideburns. He walks towards us with his hand extended and shakes my hand first and then Libby's. I notice she holds onto his hand for a moment longer than necessary and he smiles at her. I can already imagine the conversation we will be having on our homeward journey, when she will delight in replaying each second of the meeting.

There is a build-up of tension as we walk along the corridor to Hugh's ward. I had taken advice from Hugh's doctor about the best way to approach this first meeting.

Having explained to the doctor about the emotional significance, we were advised to forewarn Hugh, only an hour or so before Raymond's arrival. Of course, there was an outside chance that Raymond wouldn't turn up and then the disappointment for Hugh would be impossible to bear.

I kept my earlier meeting with Hugh short, but I will never forget his expression when I told him that he was finally about to meet his son. I let him absorb the news.

'He's coming to see you, Hugh. He'll be here in about an hour.' I held his hand as I spoke and could feel it trembling. The young nurse who had been so kind to me when Hugh was last in hospital, was in attendance, monitoring Hugh's breathing. The oxygen mask had to remain in place, so he wasn't able to speak, but the brightness in his eyes told me everything I needed to know. Hugh may have made mistakes in his life, he may have made bad decisions, but over the months I have worked for him I've grown fond of him. I am certain Poirot's advice would be to avoid emotional attachments when working on a case, as you never know who may turn out to be the culprit. Blame can be laid at the doors of Dorothy and Hugh, and even poor Winifred. However, it strikes me the real victim is Raymond. A young man who had to grow up never knowing his father. At least it isn't too late to put that right.

Chapter 28

In the end, there is no crime to present to DS Bright. I am certain a crime has been committed, not just the probable theft of the brooch, but the way Dorothy used threats to obtain money from Hugh. But as Poirot would confirm, to bring a case to court, I need to present the police with concrete evidence and that is sorely lacking.

With the case all wrapped up I can finally relax. On my return from the hospital, I have a long soak in the bath, then wrap my favourite fluffy dressing gown around me and pad down to the sitting room, where Greg presents me with a mug of hot water and lemon.

'So, what about the brooch? Did you find out if she sold it?' he asks.

'Dorothy wouldn't tell me, but I guess she sold it and spent the money years ago.'

'And that Furness chap carries on paying out all that money, every month. It's incredible his wife didn't notice.'

'It sounds as though they were quite well off. I think there was money from his wife's family and I suppose Hugh took charge of all the finances. That's the way things were done back then.'

'Sounds like an excellent plan,' Greg says, trying to keep a straight face.

'Don't go getting any ideas. In fact, let me go and check the tea caddy, see if the three pounds, four shillings and tuppence is still there.'

Every week we each put money in the tea caddy and every few months we choose a treat to splash out on. Last month it was the Beatles' *Abbey Road* album, which is now playing on repeat in the background.

'And to keep a son from knowing his father, I can't believe a mother could be so cruel.'

'Well, it's like Frank Bright said to me ages ago, you see the worst of human beings in this job.'

'I'm guessing you don't mean the library,' Greg says, with a cheeky grin. 'Speaking of jobs, has he paid you like he promised?' Greg says.

'Yep, and that is most definitely not going into the tea caddy.' I put my hands on my midriff and pretend to whisper, 'Bean, tomorrow we'll go out and order your *Silver Cross* pram, shall we?'

'Don't I get a say in it?'

'You, Mr Juke, will be responsible for pushing it home,' I say, laughing.

Christmas is just a couple of weeks away, giving us all more than one reason for a celebration. Having checked with everyone that they are happy to give Italian food a try, I call in to see Rosetta Summer. We settle on a Saturday evening, so that she has a few days to consider the menu and buy whatever is needed.

'We will bring a bottle of wine,' I say, but she waves her hand at me.

'No, I have kept some wine from my last visit home, for a special occasion. And this is special,' she says, beaming. 'So sad Mr Furness will not join us, but I will meet his friends.'

'It's not possible for him to be any happier at the moment, Rosetta, so don't worry about him,' I say, 'and I promise to give him a full account of our Italian extravaganza on my next hospital visit.'

Greg and I pick up dad, managing to squeeze Charlie into the back of the car. Libby brings Phyllis, who is still hobbling a little as a result of her swollen ankle, but has no hesitation about using a walking stick. As Ethel Latimer said, there isn't much that will stop Phyllis once she sets her mind to something.

When Rosetta opens the door to us an infusion of garlic, basil and oregano wafts through from the kitchen. As we walk into the dining room I notice the absence of tinsel and coloured streamers that bedeck dad's house. Instead, in the bay window, is a beautiful hand-made crib. While Libby takes control of all the introductions, I bend down to inspect the crib. The figures of Joseph, Mary and the three wise men are exquisitely hand-painted and the little baby Jesus is even wrapped in a muslin swaddling cloth. Rosetta has positioned the crib on the window seat that fills the bay and has the curtains pulled back, allowing the warm yellow streetlight to shine over the nativity scene, as a reminder of the Star of Bethlehem.

It has me so entranced I miss Libby's questions, which have resulted in Rosetta telling us all about her homeland. According to Libby, it is the one country she has always wanted to visit. It's the first I have heard of it, but as Rosetta's face lights up as she chatters away, I realise Libby has done exactly the right thing to kick-start the evening.

'Your nativity scene is perfect,' I say. 'Where did you get it?'

'I bring it from my home,' she says, beaming. 'A little bit of Puglia in Tamarisk Bay.'

I walk dad over to the bay window and describe the crib to him, promising that by next year we will have one just as beautiful, even if I have to make it myself. 'Can you imagine,' I say, feeling the thrill of anticipation as I speak, 'it will be Bean's first Christmas.'

'Don't rush the months away. Your little one might even be crawling by then,' Phyllis says, having overheard our conversation. 'So, you can forget about hanging

Christmas baubles. The whole lot will be on the floor before you know it.'

'Rosetta, in a few days' time my Aunt Jessica is visiting,' I tell her, as she pours drinks for us all. 'I'd love you to meet her. She has spent the last few years in Italy, I don't know which region, but perhaps she will know about your home town?'

'It would be wonderful to talk about Italy with your *Zia*. Does she make only a short visit?'

'We don't really know. We have years to catch up on and it seems we will also be meeting her friend,' dad interjects, with an emphasis on the last word.

'It is not a surprise if she has found love in Italy, it is the country of *amore*,' Rosetta says, beaming.

'All we know is that his name is Luigi,' I say.

'Another mystery for you, perhaps?' Rosetta says with a wink. We take our seats around the dining table, ready for a starter of salami and olives. It's my first experience of both and Greg explodes with fits of laughter at the face I pull when I bite into the first olive.

'Ugh,' I exclaim, when the bitterness of the dark flesh hits my tongue.

'You will get used to it,' Rosetta says, smiling.

'Er, no, I don't think I will,' I say, surreptitiously returning the other untasted olives to the central dish.

I manage to get my own back when we launch into the main course. I delight in watching Greg and Libby struggle to wind the spaghetti around their fork, with sauce being splashed everywhere, but Phyllis shows us all up with her masterful manipulation of the wriggling strands. To save any embarrassment for dad, I cut his up, but then proceed to make as bad a job of eating my own and Rosetta watches on amused.

'It is not hard,' she says, 'you do it like this.' Using just a fork, she twizzles the spaghetti around in the plate, gathering a perfect quantity so that once it reaches her mouth it is popped in without any mess or trouble.

The chatter is lively and comfortable. Now and then I glance over at Rosetta. She is like the proverbial cat with the cream, completely in her element, revelling in the company and an opportunity to immerse herself once more in the tastes and smells of her homeland.

A couple of hours later and we are all replete. The men have enjoyed Rosetta's *vino rosso* and Phyllis surprises us by announcing that she has spoken to the Central Library manager about helping out with the library van, starting in January.

'Don't think you can take a back seat, though,' she tells me, with a wink. 'I'll drive and you can do the rest.'

'Sounds like a perfect deal to me,' Greg says, a little too enthusiastically.

Before I can get into a conversation about driving, Libby intervenes. 'Janie has an important task to accomplish before we have dessert.'

Everyone turns to look at me and for a moment I'm not sure what she is expecting of me. Then I remember.

'Ah, yes, finally I get the chance to use this,' I say, pulling my camera from my bag. For the next ten minutes I fuss around, positioning everyone for various group shots. While I am in the middle of snapping away, Libby takes the camera and holds my hands out in front of her to study my fingers. 'Is it working?' she asks.

'See for yourself.'

'I'll give you eight out of ten for effort. Your nails are still a bit scruffy for my liking, but I reckon the varnish is doing some good. Just keep it up, okay?'

'Yes, boss.'

'Now, let me take a picture of you and Bean before its arrival?' she says.

'One of mum, dad and Bean, I think,' I reply, grabbing Greg's hand.

The end of the evening comes too soon, but I have to admit to being the first to flag a little. We say our goodbyes and Libby and Phyllis follow us out to the cars.

'Okay, I've decided,' Libby says, giving me a hug. 'The money you kindly gave me, I know what I'm going to use it for. I'm booking a trip to Roma and with that extra money I'll be able to really see the sights. Fancy joining me?'

Greg sidles up to us, takes my hand and squeezes it and, in unison, we both reply, 'maybe next time. We have a baby to plan for, remember?'

With my newly developed photos in my duffel bag I make my way to the hospital. If Raymond is visiting I will make my excuses and disappear, but as I approach Hugh's bedside there are no visitors and his oxygen mask is still in place. This might be a one-sided conversation, but I've come to recognise his expressions over the time I've known him, so body language will tell me all I need to know. For the moment he is dozing, his eyes gently closed and his breathing steady. The frown that had become an almost permanent feature has dissipated. I sit and watch him for a while, imagining that first meeting between him and Raymond, his only child. I hold my hands over my bump and whisper to Bean. 'We are so lucky, you, dad and me. The three of us will be indomitable, caring and sharing, with no secrets and no lies.'

The sheets rustle as Hugh wakes and turns his head towards me.

'Hello,' I say, wishing I could give him a hug. 'How are you feeling?'

He gives me a thumbs-up and smiles.

'It's been quite a journey, hasn't it? I've brought some photos to show you the celebratory supper we had in your honour. It's just a shame you couldn't be there.'

I take the photos and lay them out on his bedspread. He picks each one up to examine them more closely.

'As you can see, we all struggled with the spaghetti. Except for Rosetta, of course. She is the only one who doesn't have spaghetti sauce down her front. Phyllis did rather well too. I have a feeling she might have been to Italy at some point, when she was young maybe.'

He gives me a quizzical look.

'Phyllis? She's Libby's grandmother, part of the Janie Juke mystery solving team,' I say, winking at him. 'You're thinking there's bound to be a few interesting anecdotes that I need to coax out of her, aren't you?'

He nods, lifts his hand and removes his oxygen mask.

'We are all coloured by our experiences, that's for sure,' he says, his voice barely a whisper.

'You shouldn't take that mask off, we'll have Sister shouting at both of us if we're not careful.'

'I want to thank you.'

'It's funny but when I took on your case I was pleased to earn some extra money and honoured that you believed in me and my abilities. But the best reward of all is knowing you and Raymond have found each other.'

He nods and smiles.

'I don't need to ask you how it was when you first saw him, I can imagine it all too well. And what about Dorothy, do you think you can ever forgive her?'

He shrugs his shoulders and gestures to his bedside locker. 'In the drawer,' he says.

I slide open the drawer and inside, on top of the Bible, is a postcard with a photo of a fighter plane on one side. I hand it to Hugh, he turns it over and gives it back to me.

'*You will always be my hero, dad. Your son, Raymond,*' I read it out to Hugh and then give him the card back.

'Winnie,' he says, his voice now fading.

'You wish Winnie could have met him, don't you?'

He nods and wipes away the tears that are appearing at the corner of his eyes, tears of mixed emotions, sadness, relief, joy.

'Put the mask back on, Hugh, save your energy. I'll stay for a while until you're ready to sleep.'

I watch him as he closes his eyes and drifts off into a peaceful slumber. Hugh's troubles started before I was even born. Dorothy brought him years of anguish, but if he had never met her he wouldn't have Raymond. Good things coming from bad. He has waited half a lifetime to meet his son. We have just a few months before we meet our precious child. I lay my hands on my midriff and enjoy the sensation of Bean moving around inside me.

Thank you

As part of my research for the book I contacted The Keep, which provides a wonderful archive of East Sussex records: **www.thekeep.info/collections/** They helped to ensure the details about Janie's library van was as accurate as possible. Sussex Police were able to confirm the back story for Janie's father, Philip, all made sense.

In *Lost Property* it was vital that the information relating to the Second World War and the Special Operations Executive was authentic and for this I am enormously grateful for the advice I received from Tangmere Military Aviation Museum:

www.tangmere-museum.org.uk/

I was able to immerse myself in wartime anecdotes by reading through the BBC World War Two archives - *The People's War:*

www.bbc.co.uk/history/ww2peopleswar/

Most authors will agree that writing can be a lonely pursuit. So I consider myself very fortunate to have the encouragement and support of some wonderful people. Janie might have withered along the way if it were not for them. My brilliant writing buddies, Chris and Sarah, and my brother, David, continue to offer me not only invaluable critiques, but inspiration to keep going. Heartfelt thanks also go to family and friends too numerous to list here. I am grateful to you all.

And, in the words of one of my favourite songs, my love and thanks go to my husband Al, who is *'the wind beneath my wings'.*

If you enjoyed *Lost Property,* turn the page to read an extract from Isabella Muir's third Sussex crime novel

The Invisible Case

It's 1970 and Tamarisk Bay is preparing for its first Easter of the decade, while a certain family is preparing for a homecoming...

Chapter 1

Tuesday - platform 18, Roma Termini

If it had been an ordinary day Jessica might have noticed the briefcase. Was it there, tucked under one arm, as he extended his other to shake her hand? Over the coming days she frequently reflected back to that moment. She replayed it again and again, but all she could remember were the sights and sounds she was leaving behind.

The train for Paris was due to leave at noon. They both arrived early, with twenty minutes to spare before the start of their journey. It had been a while since she had seen Luigi and as he walked towards her on the station platform she was struck by his aquiline features, the way his hair fell forward over his eyes, despite him constantly brushing it back with his hands. He was maybe six inches taller than her so as he approached her she found herself looking up at him. His eyes weren't focused on her, they looked beyond her into the distance.

A porter walked behind Luigi, pushing a steel-framed trolley laden with luggage. Luigi held his hand up, indicating they had arrived at the right carriage. The porter unloaded two cases from the trolley, setting them beside Luigi's feet, then hovered, waiting for the inevitable tip. Luigi stuffed his hand in a trouser pocket, grabbing a handful of lire and thrust it at the man with the briefest of nods. Then Luigi turned towards Jessica. 'All your life in one suitcase and a small holdall?'

'Travelling light,' she replied, with a shrug and a girlish laugh.

'It's good to see you again. And thank you.'
'What for?'

'For letting me tag along.'

The cacophony of Italian voices meant they had to shout to be heard. Each of the thirty-two platforms at Roma Termini buzzed with comings and goings. Friends laughing as they ran along the platform, arm in arm. A husband hugging his wife before waving her off with a loud '*Ti amo*'. It was an orchestra of sound; trolley wheels that needed oiling, loud conversation, even music, all combining to make it difficult to pick out the tannoy announcement that the Paris train was preparing to leave. The language itself wasn't a problem for Jessica. She'd mastered more than the basics since she'd been living in Italy. But the announcer's voice was incoherent, muffled by the station's loudspeakers.

An elderly man tipped his hat to Jessica as he passed, on his way to join a queue at the mobile food and drink stands. Then she quickly moved to one side as a railway worker brushed past her with a broom in his hand. Not just noise, but movement all around her. Being a part of it made her heart race a little. It reminded her why she loved travelling, she had been still for too long.

'Having second thoughts about leaving?' Luigi moved past her to load his cases into the carriage.

'It's different for you, you were born here.'

'But you're going home, to your family.'

'Yes, and it's the right thing to do, but it doesn't mean I won't miss every bit of it.'

'The sunshine?'

'More than that, but yes, I'll be swapping a stroll by the port under an azure sky for grey clouds and April showers.'

She stopped speaking to listen to an exchange between two men, their voices gruff and forceful. One of the men raised his arms in the air, a conductor commanding his orchestra.

'The first time I watched two Italians having a conversation I thought they were arguing.' The memory made her smile. 'I was convinced they were about to start a fight in the street. Instead, it turned out they were discussing the best way to cook ravioli. It's their passion I'll miss, for food, wine, football...'

'Family?'

'Of course family.' One end of Jessica's scarf was caught by a gust of wind. She took the scarf off, rearranged it, then wrapped it around her neck again, tucking both ends into the collar of her blouse. 'Listen to me rambling on, just ignore me. Anything for the journey before we leave? Water, fruit?'

'No, nothing. Let's get settled.'

They moved along the corridor towards their compartment.

'I have 6D,' Luigi said, glancing at his ticket, before sliding open the door, pushing his cases ahead of him. His tall muscular frame made light work of lifting them both onto the luggage rack. He turned to Jessica. Her scarf was caught under the strap of her shoulder bag and she was struggling to untangle it. 'Let me help.'

'People will think I'm taking advantage.'

He raised an eyebrow.

'Young man, older woman,' she said. 'Anyway, I can manage, thanks.'

'Not so young. I'll be thirty next week.'

'Practically on your way to middle age,' she said and laughed.

They swapped seats so that she could sit beside the window, but by the time the train pulled out of the station Luigi had turned to his newspaper, Jessica to her book. There was a long journey ahead.

A family of four joined the train at Bologna, bursting into their carriage with energy and noise. The Italian mother ushered her husband and two young sons into their seats, before sharing out several bags of food among them. They tucked into thick slices of Italian bread, interleaved with *mortadella*. She gave them each a tomato cut into pieces and Jessica watched as the children trickled its juice over the bread. There was an orange each to follow, expertly peeled, the fine spray of zest filling the air in the carriage with the aroma of the Mediterranean. As she breathed it in, Jessica thought of all the early mornings she had strolled through the fruit and vegetable markets, the stalls piled high with ripe peaches, golden apricots and juicy cherries. The smells would linger on her clothes, so that in the evening she would shake out a shawl or a scarf and enjoy the perfume all over again.

'Passaporti, passaporti.' The passport official made his way through the train several hours later as they approached the Italian-Swiss border.

Jessica ferreted in her bag and handed her passport to the thick set man, who looked uncomfortable in his uniform, the buttons a little too tight. His cap was perched so precariously on his head it seemed a jerk of the train would send it toppling. The official looked at Luigi's passport first, he had thrust it at him in an almost defiant manner.

'Now there's a man who looks distinctly disenchanted with his job,' Jessica whispered, once the official had left the compartment.

'We can't all love what we do.' Luigi turned back to his newspaper, holding it in such a way that the child sat beside him wouldn't disturb him each time he fidgeted. The boy, who was around seven or eight, was enamoured with a toy car. He spun the wheels, running it over the palm of his hand.

'What about you?' Jessica persisted, trying to strike up a conversation. 'Did you enjoy working for Mario?'

'Bar work is okay.'

'Plenty of tips? My bar work in Crete earned me more in tips than I got in wages.' Jessica held her hands out towards the little boy, pointing to the toy car. He handed it to her and she made a show of inspecting it before handing it back.

'Are you hoping to find work in England, Luigi?'

'I don't know how easy that would be.'

'Tamarisk Bay isn't unlike Anzio, a bit smaller maybe. At least that's how I remember it, but it's nine years since I lived there. There's usually plenty of seasonal work to be had and you're arriving at start of the season. But London isn't far away. I thought you might want to seek the bright lights of the city?'

'That's not why I'm going to England.' Luigi turned back to his newspaper.

'Did you see the way that man looked at us when we handed over our passports?'

'Disgruntled?'

'No, something else. Inquisitive maybe.'

Luigi shrugged. 'It's not unusual for friends to travel together. He seemed very interested in you. Perhaps he fancies himself an English wife?'

'Now you're teasing me.'

'You're still young enough not to be invisible.'

'Thanks, I think.'

It was early evening when the attendant pulled down the beds in each compartment. If Jessica had followed her brother into the army the bedding that was handed out might have reminded her of those days. There was little appeal in the solid pillows and rough grey blankets.

'Not exactly first class,' Jessica said.

'You're too fussy, stretch out for a while, it doesn't matter if you don't sleep. Rest your eyes, at least.'

The family settled onto their bunks with little fuss. Perhaps they were frequent travellers, used to the transition from day to night in this little travelling hotel room. The father soon began to snore. The two boys top and tail on one bunk, occasionally complained when one kicked the other. The mother had her back to Jessica and each time one of her sons moved she shushed them back to sleep.

Making as little noise as possible, Jessica eased the door open and stepped out into the corridor. Several passengers were standing, others were sitting on their cases, taking advantage of the cheaper tickets that offered a journey, but no seat. She had done the same thing in the past, to save a few lire. She peered through the grimy windows at the jagged shapes of the mountains, made more eerie in the moonlight. In several hours the sun would rise and they would be beyond the Alps and heading for France.

In the corridor she slotted herself into a space between a young woman and a burly man. The man was resting his head against the window. The woman reminded Jessica of herself years ago, when she first set off on her European adventure. Leaving Philip and Janie had been a wrench, but it was the right time for them and for her. Now she was heading back to them.

Once the dawn started to break, the milky light filled the carriage. The man beside her looked up from the window and turned his head from left to right, trying to ease out the stiffness in his neck. Jessica caught the gaze of the young woman and they both spoke simultaneously, causing a quiet laugh from each of them. The girl introduced herself as Cinzia, going on to explain she was travelling to England; it would be her first time outside Italy. Friends had told her it was bitterly cold in England and it rained every day. Jessica went to reassure her, but the door to the compartment slid open, interrupting their chatter.

'Breakfast?' Luigi asked.

'Good idea,' Jessica replied, 'but I need to freshen up first.' Moving back into the compartment she took her holdall down from the luggage rack. The family had also started to stir, the children asking for food, the father grumbling that it was too early to be thinking of their stomachs. Jessica rifled through her holdall, pulling out her washbag and a sweater, before making her way to the small toilet at the end of the carriage. Once she had washed, brushed her teeth and put on a sweater, she studied herself in the small mirror, above the washbasin. Sweeping her dark auburn waves away from her face she ran her fingers across the fine lines circling her eyes. She had always been freckly, but after nine years in southern climes the freckles had taken over. '*More speckled hen than elegant swan,*' she thought, laughing at her reflection. She applied a lick of mascara and a smear of lipstick, then she was ready to greet the day. 'You'll do,' she said, stuffing everything back into her washbag and returning to the compartment.

The train seemed to speed up as they made their way along the corridor to the dining car. A couple of times Jessica bumped her shoulder against one of the compartments, feeling guilty in case she disturbed travellers who were still sleeping. With the blinds down on most of the doors and windows it was a guessing game as to whether the occupants were awake. As the train swerved around a tight bend Luigi, who was ahead of her, stumbled, brushing up against one of the doors. The blinds on the door were pulled up, revealing two travellers, a man and a woman, sitting opposite each other by the far window. The man's face with partly covered by his hat, which he had pulled forwards over his eyes, perhaps finding it more conducive to sleep. Luigi stopped so suddenly that Jessica walked into him.

'Watch out,' Jessica said, 'we nearly ended up on the floor.'

There was no reply, instead Luigi was focused on the two people in the compartment.

'Move along, we're creating a hold up,' Jessica said, as two more passengers came along the corridor behind her.

A few minutes later they were seated in the dining car. There were three other tables in use, nevertheless the waiter seemed to be preoccupied with polishing the cutlery on the vacant tables. After a short wait he took their order and returned with a pot of freshly brewed coffee and a basket of warm croissants; the smells arriving at their table before the waiter placed them down in front of them.

Jessica broke the silence. 'You look as though you've seen a ghost.'

Luigi took a croissant from the basket and tore it into pieces, grabbing a paper serviette from the container in the centre of the table to wipe his hands. 'I thought I recognised the man in the compartment back there.'

'You should have said, we could have stopped. Catch him on the way back maybe.' She poured herself a coffee and offered the pot to Luigi. 'That's a coincidence, bumping into someone you know.'

'I'm probably imagining things.'

'I thought I was the one who hadn't slept.'

Luigi emptied his coffee cup and looked up, hoping to catch the attention of the waiter for a fresh pot. 'Have you told your family about me?'

'They know I am bringing a friend.'

'What else do they know?'

'What else is there?'

The train swerved a little. The coffee slopped about, spilling into the saucers.

'Another croissant?' Jessica handed the basket to her companion.

'No, I've had enough. We should return to our carriage soon. I'm uncomfortable leaving our things unattended.'

'Who's going to be interested in our belongings? They certainly won't find any treasures among my bits and pieces.' She drained the last remnants of coffee and pushed the cup away, mildly irritated by Luigi's fingers drumming on the tablecloth.

'Tell me again what your brother is like,' Luigi said.

'He's kind, clever and...'

'He's older than you, isn't he?'

'Yes, a few years.'

The finger drumming stopped for a moment, only to start again as he asked, 'Has his blindness changed him?'

'He's resilient, tenacious. It wasn't just the accident. He had to deal with his wife walking out and then having to look after Janie. He is a force to be reckoned with.'

'Sounds as though your memory of your brother is coloured?'

Jessica looked askance at Luigi, surprised by what sounded like an accusation.

'Rose-tinted is the phrase, isn't it?' he continued. 'A younger sister looking up to her big brother.'

'I lived with him for several years as an adult, there was nothing childlike about those times. He was a good man. He is a good man.'

'But it's years since you last saw him. He may have changed.'

'I know my brother. He won't have changed. Not in the way you are suggesting. Not for the worse. You're passing judgement when you don't know anything about my family and precious little about me.'

'I don't mean to offend you. It's just that there are layers to a person that can remain hidden. Their thoughts, their fears, their past.' Luigi shifted in his seat, looking around at the other people in the dining car, before refocusing on Jessica. 'And he fought in the war, in Italy? You said he was in Anzio for a time?'

'I don't think he fought. He drove trucks, ferrying goods around the place, vital supplies, that sort of thing. To be honest, it's not something he talks much about, so I don't know the details. But yes, he spent some time in Italy and he mentioned Anzio. It was fascinating to think he might have walked the same streets I walked. But back then it wasn't the Anzio you and I know. Anyway, you'll be able to ask him yourself soon enough. Don't be surprised though if he doesn't open up. People don't like to talk about their war experiences, it wasn't exactly a time of joy.'

She stood, taking her shoulder bag from the seat. 'I need to go back now, I've got a rotten headache. Lack of sleep, I suppose.'

As they made their way back to their compartment, the passport official pushed past them and on into the dining car.

'I'm surprised to see him still on board. I thought he hopped on, checked documents and got off again at the next station,' Jessica said, once the uniformed man moved away from them.

'Perhaps he is hungry,' Luigi replied wryly.

As they made their way along the corridor Jessica slowed, so this time Luigi almost bumped into her. 'This is your friend's compartment, isn't it? Looks like he's popped out,' she said, trying not to stare at the woman who was now on her own and looking mildly perturbed at the level of interest from two passing strangers. 'It's a shame you've missed a chance to speak to him, maybe drop back in a while and see if he's around.'

Luigi shrugged and continued walking, brushing past Jessica.

Once they were back in their own compartment, there was no sign of the Italian family, just a few crumbs left on one of the seats, leading Luigi and Jessica to assume they had got off at the last stop. The couchettes had been turned back into seats and the bedding collected.

'Ideal opportunity to rearrange my things.' Jessica said, pulling her suitcase from the luggage rack and opening it out on one of the seats. She smoothed out her clothes to make a fresh space for her washbag, which she had stuffed into the top of her holdall. She squashed it into one corner of her suitcase, closed the case and turned to Luigi. 'Give me a hand to lift it back up?'

As he raised the case above his head towards the rack, he paused, a frown creasing his forehead. 'Wait,' he said, putting the case back down onto the seat.

'What?'

They stood side by side, Luigi staring at the luggage rack and Jessica staring at his face, which was become paler by the second. For a moment she thought he might faint.

Then he grabbed the remaining luggage from the rack, thumping it down on the floor in an almost feverish panic.

Each of them had brought coats that they had laid over the cases, but now he threw these onto the seat.

'What on earth is the matter?' she said, holding tight to her shoulder bag, fearing this would be the next thing he might want to grab.

He glared at her, banging a fist against the side of the train compartment.

'My briefcase, it's gone.' He stopped moving and stood with his arms outstretched as if pleading for someone to magic the situation away.

'What do you mean it's gone?'

'It's not there, Jessica. It's been stolen.'

The Invisible Case is available in paperback, or on Kindle from Amazon.

Lightning Source UK Ltd.
Milton Keynes UK
UKHW041916180419
341266UK00001B/76/P